MURDER

FOR A MOMENT

THE WICHITA P.D. SERIES, BOOK #1

DONALIE BELTRAN

MURDER FOR A MOMENT

ISBN-10: 0-9896362-7-5
ISBN-13: 978-0-9896362-7-8

Available in paperback and eBook

Published by: Killing Time Press, LLC

DEDICATION

This book is dedicated to my beautiful mother, Blanche Tuxhorn. She is my joy and inspiration. Without her, this series would not have happened.

Thank you, Mom, for your constant support for my unquenchable desire to write.

Hey, Mom, I love you *more!* ☺

ACKNOWLEDGMENTS

I would like to thank every member of the Wichita Police Department for their service and the sacrifices they make every day to keep us safe. Although it may not seem like it at times, most of the people you protect are very grateful.

My family and I have the upmost respect for what police officers do and the dangers they face every day. Our prayers go with you.

God bless you all.

CONTENTS

MURDER FOR A MOMENT

CHAPTER

1

"911—What is your emergency?"

"This is Pastor Tim Stanton of the Trinity Pentecostal Church. I need to report a dead man in my church."

~~~

When Wichita Police Detective Donna Decker showed up at the church, the place was alive with flashing squad-car lights and two-way radios blaring.

...ksssssh...footprints...ksssssh...Copy that...What... ksssshhh... Will look...kssssssshh... Say again? ...ksssssh.

Thursday night seemed an odd time for a church to be open, but who was she to say? Her church, on the east side of Wichita, was often open odd days for some special event or another. Was death a special occasion?

"Guess so...," she muttered, barely out loud.

It was eight in the evening and the sun had departed, taking with it any sign of natural light. The streetlamps were vying for a weak second. However, every light in the church was ablaze, making it appear a mini-sun had stepped inside. That left the rest to run toward it, gravitating from the dim to the dazzling. Light does that to you.

Late October in Kansas, the sun sets at around seven. Donna was grateful for the extended Daylight Savings Time in recent years. But there was only a week remaining in DST, and then the curtains would close about six.

The day had been beautiful. Autumn was her favorite time of year. When temps hovered around sixty-five to seventy degrees during the day and dropped to "sweater weather" at night, it didn't get any better than that. Was there a place on earth that maintained those temperatures year round? She would be very tempted to move if she found one.

Looking up at the sign above the church, it gave the name and then said, "Where the complete message of the Cross is preached." Wondering what that meant, she made a mental note to ask the pastor of this church, if she got a chance.

The layout of the church was unusual. The parking lot was on the side of the church, since the front was close to the street. Both front and back doors exited to the same side parking lot, one close to the street and the other toward the rear of the building.

There was a cool breeze. Decker's long dark hair flew over her face several times. Grabbing it, she pulled it back into a pony tail with a band she kept in her jeans pocket. Her bright blue eyes searched to see who was present.

Looking up and down the street, she took in the vehicles. Small crowds of people gathered across the street at the mobile home park. They were watching the mass of flickering blue-and-red lights, accompanied by the intense concentration of their tax dollars at work.

Was there someone sitting in that car about a block away? Watching them? Hard to tell. What type of car was it, a small SUV maybe? Another crime yuppie or something else?

Yellow crime tape was being run all around them, and Donna ducked under to get inside the perimeter. Something made her turn around again, and the car she had seen was no longer there. It didn't feel right, and she made a mental note to put it in her report.

The thought struck her funny. Sure, she will put it in her report. *Car a block away from crime scene. Don't have info on car or the person behind the wheel. Car left. Wow. That's incriminating as all get out!* Cars came and went from crime scenes all the time—that doesn't make them important. Still, something about it she didn't like.

Decker knew she wasn't the first female homicide detective on the force by any means but one of the youngest at thirty-three years of age. She'd graduated from Kansas State University with a BA in Sociology, with an emphasis on Criminology. From there she'd returned to Wichita for her Master's in Criminology at Wichita State.

She didn't intend to become a police officer. Her degrees could have taken her in many different directions, as well as to better-paying careers. Donna just seemed drawn to it.

Starting out with a beat, she rose through the ranks due to her special knack for putting the pieces of criminal puzzles together. She had been a detective for over a year now and had excelled. No one could deny her ability to solve a case.

Finding her six-foot-two-inch partner, Lou McGregor, standing next to the back door, talking to a man just as tall was an unusual sight. Heading his way, she felt small next to Lou and this stranger, even appearing five-seven in her two-inch-heel boots

Lou always amazed her. He gave "tall, dark, and handsome" a new meaning. At thirty-eight, he had been a detective for four years. The only problem she'd had working with her light-skinned African-American partner was his live-in girlfriend, Clarissa Waters.

Donna had met her a few times. Pretty, with medium-black skin, Lou said she clung to him and that made him uncomfortable. Clarissa was jealous of anyone and anything when she wasn't with him, including Donna. She really liked her partner, but that part of his life was none of her business as long as it didn't affect his job.

"Decker, glad you could join us. How are Brad and Betty?" Lou McGregor smiled. She had told him of her plans for dinner with her parents this evening, so she ignored his question.

"This is Tim Stanton, pastor of the church. He's the one who found the body and called it in. And before you ask, there are no security cameras here." Lou nodded toward the silver-haired man about sixty years of age.

Donna couldn't help but think she had run into a TV evangelist. Tall, slender, good looking, wearing an expensive suit and jewelry, and he had every gray hair in place. The man looked like he could be Lou's Caucasian brother.

"Pastor," she acknowledged the man. Stanton? That name struck a chord, but she couldn't place it right this minute. Poor man looked like he had never seen a dead man in a church before. *Knock it off, Decker,* she scolded herself. *No time for jokes. The man's upset.*

"This is my partner, Detective Decker. Why don't you run through again what you've told me so far, Pastor?" Lou had a way with people and knew the man was having a hard time dealing with what he'd found.

"I, uh, I came by the church to pick up some papers to take home with me." Tim Stanton struggled to concentrate. "I forgot them last night when we had Wednesday night bible study. It's a new set of questions from Angela, our web designer. After I answer them, she puts them on the 'net for everyone to see. I forgot them... I... I just forgot them.

"I knew something was wrong when I found the front door unlocked. Then I entered and found the alarm system off, too. For a split second, I thought someone forgot to lock up the night before, but even as it crossed my mind, I knew it couldn't be true. That's when I flipped on the light switch."

"Where was the body when you found it?" Donna asked.

"Right in the middle of the aisle, right where... he... is now. I didn't touch a thing. When I saw he was dead, I left the building and called 9-1-1 on my cell.

"This is not a big place. A person would walk in the door from the parking lot and then down the aisle to the podium at the other end. The offices are in back." The pastor said.

"Were any lights on? Did you expect anyone to be here? Were you meeting anyone?" Lou jumped in with some good points.

"No. No lights. No, I wasn't expecting anyone to be here. Nothing planned until Saturday afternoon when the musicians come in to practice. How he got in, I don't know. Only a few people have a key and the alarm code, and he is not one of them."

"We want that list of names. In fact we need a list of all your members. Did you know the man?" Donna watched the pastor's face.

She was a good judge of people who like to stretch the truth for their own benefit. This man did not fit that bill. He appeared to be a straight shooter. "Appeared," but we won't rush to judgment just yet. Just because he is a pastor doesn't make him a saint. She wanted to make sure she kept that in perspective.

"Yes, I know him. He came to our church, not for long, maybe five or six months. His name is Henry Wilkerson, a businessman with numerous business interests from what I've heard him mention from time to time.

"If he ever filled out a membership card, I could get you his address and phone number. I can't promise anything. We are still small enough we don't make a big deal about 'declaring' your membership. Now and then we ask new people who want to be members to fill out a card and put it in the plate.

"I had an occasion to speak with him for a moment. Let's see, about two weeks ago. When I came to church, Wilkerson was already here, which is unusual. I come early to open things up and get the lights on and so forth.

"But there he was. Caroline was not with him, which I thought odd. Henry jumped out of his car and came over all excited to ask a question from the Bible. I was happy to oblige.

That's what I am here for." Tim was now thinking on his feet.

"Was Wilkerson present at the services last night? If so, was he with anyone?" Donna wondered if he could've stayed in the church after it closed. Seemed odd, but you never know what people will do.

"No, not here last night. Neither was his wife and daughter."

So much for that idea.

"We will have to take you downtown for your statement," Lou informed him, "so please don't leave just yet."

Stanton nodded, and the two detectives walked toward the front of the church building. They could see him making a phone call from his cell. The last they heard was, "Honey, I won't be home for a while...."

Walking into the front door, they turned to the right to face the length of the church. There they saw Dan Glover kneeling next to the body.

"What'd you find, Dan?" Lou and Dan went back about a dozen years; even were partners for a short time back in the day.

Dan, nearing retirement, was never fond of women on the force. Since he couldn't change the laws allowing such an atrocious thing, he tried to ignore them. Glover was the Police Sergeant on the night shift. He stood, glanced at Donna, then spoke to Lou.

"Pretty simple, Lou. Shot point blank in the head. Looks like a .38 but the coroner has to confirm." Dan was all business, but that is what made him a good cop.

"If you say a .38, my friend, then it was a .38." Dan knew his guns and Lou was aware of it. "What do you think happened?"

"Not really sure." Dan, now standing next to Lou, looked down at the body and then up and down the aisle. "But whoever shot him appears to have come from the podium, not the front door, judging the way he fell. So they may have been here when the Vic came in. I'm no church-goer, but isn't Thursday an odd night to be here?"

At about five-seven, what Dan lacked in height, he made up in weight. The man had to be three hundred pounds, with a belly that would make it hard to sit up close to the table. Donna tried not to picture it.

"The pastor is outside, and he says there were no meetings tonight. He came by for some paperwork and discovered the body." Donna explained, but she might as well talked to the wall. Dan didn't even look up at her. Jerk!

She was glad to see photos being taken of everything around her and requested extras taken of the area around the Vic's head. She was especially interested in Glover's remark about the angle of his fall. But, Donna wouldn't take his word for anything. The angle theory had to come from an expert. Glover isn't the only one who can ignore another police officer.

Man, she suddenly felt like a spoiled brat. *"Mommy, he won't talk to me so I'm pouting!" Sheez. Grow up, girl!*

"Nothing planned here at the church until Saturday afternoon. That means whoever did this probably wasn't expecting the Vic to be found for a couple more days. What better place to hide a crime than in an empty church!" Lou responded. At least her partner listened.

When she looked at him, he winked, knowing what she was thinking about Dan. She rolled her eyes, which made Lou almost chuckle out loud—but that wouldn't have gone over well with Dan.

Leaving Glover, Lou and Donna took the pew row to the left side wall aisle and headed to the back of the church.

The stage area looked as one would expect. A glass podium stood in the center with a Bible verse engraved on it. Behind were musical instruments, standing silent, waiting for someone to flip a switch allowing them to raise their voices again to worship God. The drums were encased in a small walled-in glass cubicle all their own, for the sake of acoustics.

Taking a narrow hall to the left of the stage brought you around to the back area where there appeared a janitor's closet and two small offices. One had a small sign marked "Pastor Tim" on the door. Donna liked the fact this pastor didn't stand on formality or ego.

A cell phone rang, and Donna realized it was Lou's. She heard him say, "Clarissa, I'm working. What do you *want?*"

Moving down the hall, she pulled on latex gloves as Lou went into the first small office. When you're on the force, putting latex gloves in your pocket when you get dressed is as natural as putting on shoes.

Next was a small restroom, leaving only a tiny area for the second office. Small and narrow, it seemed to function as a place to study or write. The only furniture was a small square table in the corner and two chairs. Desk supplies on the table made it functional. Nothing seemed to be out of the ordinary, so she moved on.

The hall ended with the side door also serving as the back door. It opened onto the back end of the side parking lot, not far from where the pastor was just a few minutes before. If anyone had left by that door, it would have been similar to leaving by the front, just further back on the property.

They backtracked to the front of the church where the coroner now leaned over the body. They knew Glover would have been told to move away, by Dr. K.

CHAPTER

2

"What's up, Doc?" Lou loved to razz Dr. Kandy Kay Scarpa, a pretty wisp of a woman, only five-foot-two and forty-ish. Everyone called her Dr. K.

She'd been a top-notch coroner in Texas when Sedgwick County was lucky enough to woo her away. She didn't come cheap, but she came anyway.

There were even rumors that a television show might be in the making for her autopsies. Donna knew Dr. K would make a terrific show, since she even called herself "The Gothic Cowgirl." That is, the Gothic cowgirl who'd married an Italian.

NCIS may have Abby with her black hair and fingernails. Wichita has Kandy Kay with her white hair and black bangs to go with the black fingernails. Oh and then there were the cowboy boots.

"Not up, Lou—down. He's down and dead." She looked annoyed, but everyone knew she had a great sense of humor. Weird, but great. Something else this job will do to you. Without a sense of humor, you wouldn't stay around very long.

"Wow, now you tell me." Lou said, feigning disappointment. "No wonder I didn't see the body!"

Donna grinned and gave Lou a nudge with her elbow for the stupid joke. Dr. K. was one of her favorite people.

"Well, guys," the doctor started. "He was shot with a .38. In fact, it is probably the one that was found under the pew."

"Whaaat? They found a gun?" Donna tried not to smirk at Lou, but she was glad Sgt. Perfect-Cop-Because-I-Am-A-Man-Glover had missed it.

"Yep. It was a .38 with a silencer on it. What do you say to a possible suicide?" Dr. K. grinned up at them both, knowing she'd just complicated their case by throwing in that possibility.

"Uh, you think he came to a church to do himself in?" Lou looked at the entire area with new eyes. Without realizing it, he added the words out loud, "Would someone get so mad at God that he would end it in His house?"

"Don't know yet. It'll take a couple of days, but you'll get my report. Probably Monday. Gang problem on the west side has the morgue filling up. Plus there was a highway accident that was added on my priority list, for whatever reason I don't know. It will most likely be Saturday before I get to him." She gave orders to her staff for moving the body to the morgue.

"When do you think he died, Doc?" Donna needed something to work on here.

"A guess? It appears sometime last night, but I can narrow it down more after the autopsy. Whatever the time, you can bet it wasn't convenient. The dead never die at a convenient time. Ever notice that?"

Donna grinned. That was Dr. K. She could come up with the strangest ideas at, well, the strangest times.

Lou perked up, "Wow! Can I quote you on that?"

Dr. K.'s deadpan face belied her humor. She came back with, "Only if you want to be one of them."

Donna burst out laughing while Lou grabbed his heart and feigned being shot.

Getting back to the business at hand, Donna turned to Lou. "Church services were over at eight-thirty. So let's say it was nine to ten o'clock before everyone left. It had to have happened after that."

Lou nodded, trying to put the timeline together in his mind. "Let's get back to the office and interview our pastor."

Donna nodded at the idea, and they left the building.

As they exited, they saw a tow truck hauling off Wilkerson's car.

Lou, Donna, and Tim Stanton got into Lou's car and headed downtown. One advantage to being a detective was being assigned an unmarked vehicle or using your own. Lou like using his own.

Donna also knew Lou didn't like driving a squad. He said the black-and-whites made him too conspicuous. He liked being unmarked. And, truth told, so did she. You get more information out of people if you don't scream "I'm the Law!" Not that it mattered tonight.

A half an hour later, they sat down in an interview room. Stanton once again told how he had forgotten the papers from the night before and decided to pick them up tonight. He thought he would have time on Friday to work on the questions, so it seemed like the thing to do.

He'd found the door unlocked and the alarm off. When he turned on the light, he could see to walk through the church to his office, and that

19

was when he saw a man lying on the floor. Not knowing what to think, he said he ran to the man and knelt down.

He was talking to him, trying to get his attention, when he saw massive amounts of blood pooled on the floor near his head and realized he was dead. It appeared he was shot in his right temple. Stanton was stunned. He stood, took a few steps backward, and then turned and left the building while reaching for his cell phone.

"The rest," he said, "is on the 9-1-1 tape."

It was well after midnight when Lou drove Tim Stanton and Donna back to their cars at the church. The pastor could finally make his way home, but Donna and Lou couldn't call it a night. At least, not yet.

There was still the detail of notifying the next of kin. In this case, it was the dead man's wife, Caroline Wilkerson.

They didn't need Stanton's information or the address. Henry Wilkerson's identification was still on him, along with almost a thousand dollars in cash. Obviously, it had not been a robbery.

Wilkerson lived in an expensive home in Eastborough, one of the original high-end areas of town. There were several such areas now, but Eastborough always gave off the impression of "old" money.

Eastborough was a small town all its own, swallowed up by Wichita many years ago. They still maintained their own police department but relied on Wichita for their Fire Department.

Since it was on the East side of Wichita, where both of the detectives lived, they decided to take their individual vehicles giving them the ability to go their separate ways after speaking with the wife.

Lou informed the Eastborough P.D. they would be in the area. After both detectives parked by the front door on the circle drive, it was Donna who rang the doorbell and heard beautiful chimes ring out.

The house was quiet, and no one responded, which was not surprising as it was now close to one o'clock, Friday morning. This wasn't information that could wait until tomorrow, so she rang the bell again. This time, a light came on somewhere upstairs. A few minutes later, a lovely woman in a robe, opened the door.

They showed her their badges and asked if they could come in. She said "Yes," but added that they would be disappointed, as Henry wasn't home. He was out of town for a couple of days.

"Could you please be seated, Mrs. Wilkerson?" Lou was being as gentle as possible. Caroline looked exhausted and confused but sat on the living room couch as she was instructed. Lou and Donna sat on the other couch, facing her.

Donna spoke first. "We are sorry to wake you, Mrs. Wilkerson. Your first name—do you go by Carol?"

"No, it's Caroline. And I had been asleep for only a few moments. I went to bed at ten-thirty, but I was listening for any breathing problems from my daughter." She stared back at them.

"When did you last see or speak to your husband, Mrs. Wilkerson?" Donna figured she might as well get right to the point.

"Uh…About four yesterday afternoon, I think. He called to say he wouldn't be home for dinner. He said he had a business meeting in Denver and had to leave right away. Why are you asking about Henry?"

"Did that happen often—his leaving on a moment's notice?" Donna pushed for more answers.

"Yes, it does." Caroline sounded tired.

"Ma'am, we are sorry to inform you your husband was found dead at the Trinity Pentecostal Church," Lou said as gently as possible.

Shocked, Caroline stammered, "What do you mean *at the church*?" She was up and pacing the floor now, unable to sit. "What do you mean *dead*?"

Donna felt sorry for her and could understand the initial denial that came with such terrible news.

"How do you know it's Henry?" It sounded like a whisper.

"Pastor Stanton was on the scene and identified him. We will have to ask you to come to the morgue in the morning, Friday, for further identity." Lou informed her.

At the mention of the pastor's name, Caroline's hand flew to her mouth. Identify Henry's body? She nodded.

"I have to ask you about your husband's attitude. Was he sad or despondent about anything? Did he suffer from depression?" Donna knew she had to ask.

Caroline shook her head "No, no, no." The denial stage didn't last long, as Caroline stopped pacing and fell apart right before their eyes. She seemed to let go. Lou jumped up and caught her before she hit the floor and carried her back to the couch.

When she stopped crying and could sit back up on her own, she apologized for her behavior.

"Ma'am, we understand. Can you tell me what Henry had been doing on Wednesday night that he would have ended up at the church?" Lou always felt bad for the family members who suffered.

"I... uh... he called and said he was leaving town Wednesday afternoon so don't expect him for dinner. I do not understand how or why he would have ended up at the church." Caroline was hesitant to go on. She got past the shock and asked, "What happened to him, Detectives? How did he die?"

"Uh, well, we don't know if it was suicide or if someone else wanted him dead, but cause of death is most likely the bullet in his temple." The words stumbled out of Lou.

Donna put it right on the table, "Where were you last night, Mrs. Wilkerson?"

Caroline didn't seem surprised by the question.

"I was here all evening with my daughter. Henry was out of town… was *supposed* to be out of town, and Shana had the sniffles, so I didn't go to the Wednesday services at church. I enjoy the mid-week service, as it is less formal, and we laugh a lot with Pastor Tim, but there was no point in making Shana uncomfortable when she wasn't feeling well or risk infecting others with her cold. She's only three years old."

"What about between midnight and eight this morning?"

25

"We both were asleep until about seven. I got up to fix Shana's breakfast. She was up thirty minutes later."

"Do you know of anyone who would want to hurt your husband?"

Before she could answer, Caroline's composure failed her again, and she sobbed.

They watched, helpless, as she cried. After several minutes, she was trying to get control back when Lou asked if she had someone who could come over and be with her. She said her sister, Tracy, wasn't feeling well, but she would call her. Caroline said Tracy was the only family she had left. They stayed with her several more minutes to make sure she could function. They would not get any more information tonight.

When they got up to leave, Donna finished with, "Don't forget to come down to the coroner's office in the morning to identify your husband." Caroline nodded.

With the hardest part of their job done, they left the Wilkerson house. They talked for a while, standing in the driveway.

"What kind of business could you be in that you had to leave for days with no warning?"

Donna couldn't wrap her mind around that one. Most women wouldn't like living that way, but Caroline didn't seem to think anything of it.

"I know. There is a bunch here that makes little sense. I want to know a whole lot more about this guy." Lou opened Donna's car door for her, then headed for his own and they called it a night.

It was a little after two in the morning, and they both were beat. Whatever happened at the church, it would still be there tomorrow, and they would get a fresh start Friday morning.

Actually that would be this morning.

MURDER FOR A MOMENT

CHAPTER

3

Tim Stanton went home after being driven back to his car at the church by the detectives. He still couldn't believe what he stumbled across in the church, but was glad he had been able to let Lily know he would be late. Her worrying about him when she didn't feel well herself, would do no one any good.

As he turned onto his middle-class block, he could see the lights still on in his house. Pulling into his garage, he turned off the car and sat there as the garage door closed behind him.

What a night it had been. Why had he gone to the church in the first place? *Oh, yeah—the list of questions.* As Tim entered his house, he wondered if he ever got that list.

Particularly protective of his church, Tim knew all pastors become personally involved, but his experience was different. Stanton wasn't hired to be a preacher at this church. He started this church himself, from scratch, eight years earlier, and has never taken a salary.

Tired of going to church and hearing the wrong message, he knew he had been called by God to tell the truth. That is where the tag line "Where the Complete Message of the Cross is Preached" came from.

The correct message was Christ dying on the cross and rising three days later that saved humanity. Not His miracles, not His teachings, not His entire life. It was His death and resurrection that saved the world. Without that, no one would be saved.

But preachers today seemed to want to whitewash the tough stuff and talk about the miracles and how perfect He was. *Audience pleasers.* That's what they were in Tim's opinion.

To get people to come through the door these days, you need a rock band for the teens and a feel-good message for the adults.

Bull! People had to know the truth! What Jesus Christ went through on the cross was not pretty. In fact it was horrifying, but nonetheless, it was the truth.

What He did was die for our sins. Nothing pretty about that. Rising from the dead three days later proved Him to be the Son of God. There you go. His death and resurrection are what saved the world. Nothing more. Nothing less.

Starting a new church is never easy. He had seven people at his first service in his basement, and most of them were his own family. More came with time, and he rented a deserted church to use on Sundays.

31

After the membership hit about one hundred, the Lord led him to a small church for sale. Wednesday night Bible study started then. With membership at almost two hundred at this point, he planned to build a new sanctuary on the back of the property and use the small church for youth services.

To have someone die in God's house was just beyond his comprehension. How Henry got into the building, however, bothered him the most. Those with security codes were people he completely trusted.

Now standing in the family room with his wife and son, he went over all he saw at the church and what the police told him. The three of them were up until almost dawn discussing the man they wish they had known better.

"Do we know of anyone who could have given him the security code? Or how someone could have stolen it?" Tim had to find out what had happened.

Both his wife and son shook their heads. He knew he would go back to the church tomorrow and change the code. Definitely a priority for Tim to get it changed the next day.

Lily said she never personally spoke with Henry but thought him to be nice looking and he seemed to be happy to be in church. She mentioned she heard him telling another man about having been saved some years back and was proud of his wife, Caroline, for finally coming to Christ at this church.

"Henry said he was saved," Lily stated, "so we know he is safe in the arms of Jesus tonight."

Tim shouted an "AMEN!" At least something good came out of this tragedy.

Gabe became more pensive but also admitted he didn't know him well. *Something about him*, he thought, *that I just didn't trust, but now is not the time to bring it up. After all, the poor man just died.*

Before calling it a night, they all bowed their heads and prayed for the man whose last breath was taken in their church.

~~~

Caroline sat on the couch for what seemed like forever after the detectives left. Henry was dead. He'd been found in the church by Pastor Tim. *I wonder what he was doing there? The pastor, that is.*

She wasn't going to call her sister tonight. Tracy wasn't feeling well. She had called last night to see if Tracy wanted to come over for dinner with her and Shana, since Henry was out of town. But Tracy had already eaten something that didn't agree with her and had become ill.

Of course, there's always the thought that, hearing the news Tracy would feel better. Caroline always felt her sister was not crazy about her husband, but she had never said anything. She could be wrong, again. The Lord knows it had happened many times before… like when she'd married Henry.

Whatever the emotional outcome, Caroline decided to wait until close to noon before calling with the news of Henry's death. The housekeeper, Heddy, could watch Shana while she went to the morgue to identify the body.

She was actually surprised at her own emotions upon hearing of his death. Why had she fallen apart so completely? It's not like there was any love lost between them. Caroline didn't know why she'd cried so hard.

Maybe it was for the marriage that could have been, or maybe it was just the shock of his sudden death. Maybe it was just the relief in realizing her nightmare was over. Who knows what goes through your mind when something like this happens?

She didn't tell the detectives that Henry had actually called Heddy to tell her he was leaving town—not her. He didn't care whether she knew or not.

Then she remembered another question that didn't get answered. Did she know of anyone who wanted to hurt Henry? She was pretty sure that the answer to that question was "Anyone who ever knew him." But, she didn't want to come across as the embittered wife. She wasn't going to allow Henry the satisfaction of ruining her life, dead or alive.

Only a few hours left to sleep before Shana got up. She would worry about it all in the morning. Not now. She was too tired to worry about anything more tonight.

~~~

Friday morning found Caroline pensive and quiet. She knew she would have to go identify the body. Not just *any* dead body— *Henry's* dead body. When she returned, she would contact her sister with the news.

Tracy was the only family she had except for her little girl, Shana. No one else would care she was now a thirty-nine year old widow. Actually, a widow for the *second* time. Unbelievable. Caroline felt she was blessed by the way things turned out, and knew she would remain single for a very long time.

Heddy arrived at the house. Although shocked by the news of Henry's death, she was as expected, happy to watch Shana. Caroline left for downtown. Her thoughts were jumbled, but she desperately tried to put them in order.

Yesterday I hated my husband. That was yesterday, right? Yeah. And a whole lot of yesterdays before that. Okay, maybe not "hate," actually, but I had a huge dislike for the person he was. Now I am going to identify his body. I think this is going to be one of my best days in years.

After reaching the precinct, a police officer escorted her down to the basement morgue and then to a large window. On the other side laid a body covered with a sheet.

The officer nodded at the woman whose name tag said "Dr. K." A strange looking woman, Dr. K. had long white hair with solid black, blunt-cut bangs. *Odd, to say the least,* thought Caroline, *but somehow she looked perfect in that setting.*

The sheet from the upper torso was removed. It was Henry, all right.

He had a large hole in the side of his head, but there was no mistaking her cold hearted husband. Last night all she could do was cry. Right now? She might as well be looking at an unattractive dress in a store window. She certainly didn't want him back.

Oh, Henry, you would be horrified to know people would be seeing you with your face all messed up like it is! It's almost funny. I shouldn't think so, but it is. There is a big hole in your head. You look like hell, and I have no doubt that is exactly where you are.

After a moment of allowing herself to indulge in her thoughts, she turned to the officer beside her and said, "Yes, that's my husband, Henry Wilkerson." The officer nodded at Dr. K., and the sheet covered the body once again.

Escorted back up to the main floor, she

was asked to write down the names and phone numbers of her sister, any close friends, and her housekeeper. Seems the police wanted to talk to anyone who knew Henry.

She was glad to leave the morgue. It was a place she had never been before and preferred not to visit again. *Life goes on, doesn't it?* But one thing did bring a smile to her face—the incredible peace in her heart. She said a silent prayer before starting her car.

Twenty minutes later she drove into her garage. Shutting off the engine, she realized that she would be able to move her bedroom back into the master suite, and that Shana's bedroom would also have to be moved out of the second master suite. *Strange how one little thing like a death could disrupt lives so much.*

Time to call Boyce's again. Knowing Bob, he will just laugh when I tell him the beds need to be moved again. The last time, he suggested I put them on wheels. I probably should have, but at least this will be the last time. Caroline chuckled.

This afternoon she would arrange for his body to be picked up at the morgue, if they were through with him, so he could be cremated.

She didn't know if that is what he wanted to have happen because he never spoke to her of personal things. That left her to make the final decision for his resting place. It made her smile.

No family funeral for this guy. Caroline doubted anyone would show up. What would she do with his ashes? Tossing them in the trash sounded like a good idea. But, whatever she did, she knew Henry wouldn't like it. That thought made her smile again.

Now to call Tracy with the news. She would also inform Tracy and Heddy they would be contacted for an interview by Wichita's finest.

"I am sure they both will be thrilled." Getting ready to enter the house from the garage, Caroline wasn't even aware she said it out loud.

CHAPTER

4

Lou walked into the precinct a little after nine, chewing on a fast-food breakfast sandwich. Donna was already at her desk, buried in some notes.

"When do you sleep, woman? I'm beat." Lou appeared to be dragging a little. "Must be age. I can't go without sleep like I used to."

"Don't get me started on your shortcomings, old man." Donna smiled. She loved teasing her partner.

"Watch it, Goldilocks, or I will turn you over to the Big Bad Wolf." Lou finished the last gulp of coffee, crushed the cup, and threw it away. "What have we got so far?"

Donna ignored the mix-up of fairy tales in Lou's remark, but she had a hard time keeping the smile from her face.

"What?" He didn't have a clue what was going through her mind.

"Nothing, Cinderella. Well, let's see. We have a man who may or may not be a member of a church. We have a man who may or may not be meeting someone there and who may or may not have been given the code to get in. And we have a man who may or may not have killed himself." Donna smiled sweetly at him.

"Piece of cake." Lou pulled up a chair to her desk and sat down. Lou's desk faced hers, but sometimes it was just easier to get on the same side to talk.

"Seriously, Lou. This had to be a murder. Wilkerson wasn't on Stanton's list of people who had the alarm code to get into the church. It's a short list, so we have to assume our murderer is on it. Right?

"Our Vic was there for a reason, and I don't think suicide was it. But why *was* he there—a church, of all places?" Donna pushed the paper toward Lou with the names of people entrusted with the alarm code.

"Appointments are already made, Lou. The first should be here in about thirty minutes, so perk up, kiddo. There's work to do."

"Okay, let's get started." Lou was glad he had picked up food for breakfast because it looked like it would be another long day, and there was no telling when their next meal might be.

The list included the pastor's wife Lily, and their son, Gabe. Outside of the family, the list included Jill and Jason Walker as well as Jerry and Wilhelmina Walker. Jerry and Jason were twins; they were musically adept and part of the Pastor's Council and musicians who played at services, as were their wives.

Last on the list was Joe Garrett, a member of the church who volunteered to clcan when he was not running his own contract maintenance company, Garrett Enterprises. When you looked at it as a whole, there were only three families and Garrett who had the code information.

Tim Stanton let everyone on the list know about the discovery in the church the night before, because they already knew they would hear from the police as members who had access to the church.

First on the agenda was the pastor's wife, Lily and her son, Gabe. Both came in together. Donna recognized Lily immediately.

"I'll take the wife, Lou. You interview the son."

Now she knew why the "Stanton" name had sounded so familiar the night before. All of the Wichita Police Department's police dogs came from the prestigious Stanton's Protection Paws, Inc., located on ten acres outside Derby, Kansas, just ten minutes south of Wichita. You couldn't get better-quality dogs than what Lily offered at her business.

At five-foot-seven, slender, with natural good looks, she was wearing little makeup because she didn't like it. Never had. Lily preferred sensible clothes and minimal jewelry.

Donna was required to take training at the Stanton facility when she first joined the force. Some complained that it was a waste of their time having to get acquainted with the way police dogs were trained, but Donna had enjoyed every minute. She couldn't believe all the work that went into training the best. It was something she would never forget.

She could hardly keep her admiration for the woman in front of her from interfering with the interview. But contain it she must.

"Mrs. Stanton, we need to confirm your whereabouts for last evening."

"Lily, please. Only my husband's mother deserves the title of 'Mrs.'" Lily smiled, but you could see she wasn't feeling too great and dealing with what might have been the remains of a case of the flu. With members of the force out with it, Donna knew it was making the rounds.

A little stuffy, Lily said, "Don't worry. I'm not infectious, at least not any more. Just a cold. I got this prescription this morning from my doctor and am feeling a little better already.

45

But don't tell him that. I accuse him of pushing drugs for a living." She chuckled.

Donna smiled and took the prescription, looked it over, and made a note for the file. She returned it to Lily, who dropped it into her purse.

"So to answer your question, I was at home last night being fed aspirin by my darling, over-protective son, Gabe. My husband or son can get sick and all is well with the world, but if I do, life as we know it comes to a stop." Lily chuckled at the thought. "Something about a mother being sick and the whole family panics."

Donna laughed out loud and said it was the same in her family.

"I can't tell you how bad we feel about Mr. Wilkerson. The whole idea of someone dying in the church, let alone one of our own…," Lily's eyes were brimming. She got ahold of herself and straightened up. "Sorry. It's still a shock."

"Lily, can you think of any way Mr. Wilkerson could have gotten the security code to the church?"

Just as she spoke, an officer knocked on the interview-room door, entered and gave

Donna a piece of paper. He left just as quickly. She read it as she listened to Lily's response.

"For the life of me, I can't. Tim and I talked about this last night. I know in my heart that those who have the code didn't give it to him—or to anyone else, for that matter. How he could have gotten it—or the key to the front door—is beyond me." Lily was shaking her head, eyebrows knitted.

"Well, it seems the front-door lock was jimmied. That is what this note is about. So we now know he didn't have a key to the door—only the code to keep the alarm from going off."

"That seems to complicate things doesn't it? If anyone had given him the code, they would certainly have given him a key to go with it. Sounds like the man stole it somehow." Lily was looking at things from her usual rational point of view, and Donna had to agree with her assessment.

"You're right, Lily. So, we're finished for now, but please know you may be called to come back in again at a later time."

Lily smiled and said, "It will not be a problem to come back again, because I am sure I will feel much better than I did this time."

They said their goodbyes, and Lily left the room just as Gabe joined her in the hall. After they were out the door, Lou and Donna compared notes. Both were given the note about the jimmied lock.

"She says she was home with Gabe," Donna put it simply.

"Same here. Gabe said his mother wasn't feeling well and that he was there taking care of her while his father was gone. He said he was trying to get aspirin down her for her cold. He spent most of his time talking about his girlfriend, Stella. Man, is that guy in love!" Lou was chuckling.

"Gabe was about as much of an open book as you can get. The spitting image of his father, he was a happy guy who seemed to love everything and everyone. And talkative! Go figure.

"We might want to talk to Stella—Stella Douglas is her name. Maybe she had it written somewhere?" Lou was talking to himself more than anyone around him and was surprised with Donna's reply.

"I doubt it, but you never know. Put her on the list. With this new info on the jimmied lock, I doubt that any of the people coming in today are involved. No one would have given him the code and not a key. But they are scheduled, so we might as well see if they have any ideas."

Next on the list were the Walkers—all of them. That would include Jill and Jason Walker and Wilhelmina with Jerry Walker, all in their mid-thirties. Donna took the first couple, and Lou took Jerry and Wilhelmina to his interview room.

As they sat down, Lou started to speak, but Jerry spoke first. "May we start with prayer, Detective? It always works out better if God is involved."

Lou, though surprised, said he didn't mind. All bowed their heads as Jerry asked for the Lord's guidance in such a serious matter. He ended with "in the Precious Name of Jesus, Amen."

Lou started to speak again, and Wilhelmina spoke. "Please, whatever you do, don't call me Wilhelmina. Just call me Willy. Everyone does!"

Wilhelmina, uh, Willy, was not a small woman, but interestingly enough, she was very attractive and well built. But no doubt about it, she would make two of Donna.

Stunned by the interview that wasn't happening, Lou was quiet for a moment to make sure there would be no more interruptions and then said, "Pastor Stanton says the two of you have a key to the church and know the alarm code. Is that correct?"

Both Jerry and Willy nodded and said. "Yes."

"Have you ever given the code out to any unauthorized party, for any reason? Maybe a long time ago?"

Jerry shook his head "No," and Willy sat straight up as if someone had put a pin in her back, "Good gracious, no! Why would anyone give out something like that to strangers? We have a fortune in musical instruments in there. Boy, we would be in a world of hurt if anyone took all of our equipment! Know what I mean?"

When asked if they knew Henry Wilkerson, Jerry said, "Yes, at least enough to say hello."

Willy appeared deep in thought and just shook her head, "Not really. I had seen him before, but he and I had never spoken or introduced ourselves. I spoke to his wife once. A lovely lady, but I have to say she had eyes that disturbed me. Almost haunted."

"Haunted? What do you mean by that?" Lou was aware how Caroline looked in the wee hours of this morning receiving the news of her husband's death, but he wouldn't call them "haunted" exactly. But, then again, maybe they were....

"Oh, I don't know. She was just one person who always seemed to be somewhere else when you talked to them. Know what I mean?" Willy was bubbly, no doubt an extroverted personality. Lou noticed Jerry was quieter. Well, they say opposites attract.

"Do you know what kind of business he was in?" Lou leaned away from personalities and more on the man's life.

"I didn't. Did you, sweetheart?" Willy looked at Jerry, who shook his head "No." Willy continued, "They both dressed really nice, so I guess whatever he did was successful. Know what I mean?"

Yes, Lou knew what she meant. He was getting a kick out of this friendly woman. She was so open and, well, bubbly. He would bet anything she was the eternal optimist. He also knew this was a dead-end road. These people weren't involved. Just another one of those times he would bet his badge on it.

He talked with them for a while longer, asking every question he could think of. Where they were from, what they liked about their church, what they thought of the good fall weather—things to kill time until Donna finished with her interview. After bantering, even Jerry entered the conversation. They were both nice people.

Lou finally smiled and excused himself, leaving them sitting in the interview room. He walked down the hall and peeked into the window where Donna was with the other Walkers. They were all laughing about something. These people were friendly, too!

He knocked on the door, opened it, and asked Donna if he could speak to her for a second. When Donna left the room, she said, "What's up?"

"Nothing, really. I wanted to see how you were doing. My couple is clean, girl. They weren't involved. I have exhausted about every question I can think of. They are just nice people who go to the same church as the dead guy." Lou didn't want to keep them there any longer than he had to.

"I agree. Jill and Jason didn't even know the guy. Both were a little shy at first, but they really are nice people, too, when you get them started." Donna smiled just thinking about her interview.

"Then let's move on." Each returned to their interview rooms and told everyone to go home.

The whole family was laughing and waving while they said their goodbyes to the detectives on the way out.

Lou and Donna got ribbing about their "happy murder suspects" but took it in stride.

MURDER FOR A MOMENT

CHAPTER

5

Tracy Lynn Andrews walked into the precinct for her appointment. Donna showed her to room two and then got her a soda. Lou didn't have a separate interview of his own, so he joined the women, and they all got comfortable.

"Sorry about your brother-in-law, Ms. Andrews." Lou wanted to make her as comfortable as possible.

"Yes. I couldn't believe it when my sister called me earlier. Suicide? In a church? How creepy!" Tracy appeared to be fighting with the entire image of it all.

"We don't know it is suicide yet. We haven't ruled out homicide. How well did you know Henry?"

"I moved to Wichita about five years ago, to be closer to my sister. I am a mystery writer, which can be done from anywhere. Henry was traveling a lot at that time.

"Caroline was moving everything into their new Eastborough home and planning a wedding. I literally met the man on their wedding day. There were a few days I wondered if the man would even be back in town for the wedding. He had made himself scarce. It was like he was avoiding everything and left it on Caroline's shoulders." Tracy shook her head in disgust.

"I helped as much as I could; setting up times for Boyce to collect things from her place, then Henry's place, then to the new place...."

"Boyce? Boyce's Moving Service?" Lou knew who she was talking about, but Donna didn't.

"Yeah, they're here in Wichita. Caroline won't let anyone else touch her stuff. Boyce is the one she calls, no matter what has to be moved, or where. Bob's a nice man.

"Anyway, I was at the new place having everything placed where she wanted it. I couldn't help with the wedding, though. That had to be whatever Caroline wanted.

"This wedding was really important to her and I understood why. She had been married once before to a wonderful guy, Air Force Lt. Aaron Baxter. He was stationed here at McConnell Air Force Base when 9/11 happened. He was sent overseas, where he was killed 11 months later.

"Caroline was devastated. Those two were so much in love. Widowed at twenty-three, I was really worried about her back then. But, of the two of us, Caroline is the strong one. She got her life back on track and went on. It was years, though, before she would even think about dating. I guess she thought Henry would love her the same way Aaron did. Isn't that what husbands are supposed to do?" Tracy let go of a deep sigh and stared at the floor for a while.

After a moment, Donna asked, "When was the last time you saw Henry?"

"Last Sunday, I believe, at church. I don't go there very often, but when Caroline really begs, I try to make it. I am not as wrapped up in God as she is. I just haven't seen how He has shown any kindness to me." Tracy shrugged her shoulders and gave a little smile.

"I hear that." Of course, that was Lou speaking. Donna gave him a dirty look, and he sheepishly stared down at the floor.

Donna faced Tracy again and said, "What did you think of your brother-in-law?"

"What did I think of Henry...?" Tracy looked up to the ceiling, lost in thought. "If you mean did I think he was a rotten excuse for a man and a first-class jerk for the way he treated my sister? Yes, I certainly did."

Donna glanced at Lou with a look of surprise.

Lou chuckled and said, "Okay, I take it you didn't like the guy. Can you be more specific?"

"Okaaaay. Well, how about Caroline got pregnant four years ago and Henry went ballistic? He didn't want any children and wanted her to get an abortion! Can you believe that? Well, Caroline was horrified and refused." Tracy's voice was filled with disgust.

"What about after the baby was born?" Donna had taken a real dislike to this man, dead or alive.

"What about it? He was not there when she was born. He traveled more and more so he wouldn't have to be home." Tracy's emotions got to her as she thought about that time. Tears welled up in her eyes, but she refused to let them fall.

Lou asked, "Had he been despondent lately? Depressed? Anything that would cause him to kill himself?"

"I wouldn't know. Like I said, the last I saw him was on the Sunday before he died, and that was only for a few minutes as I talked with Caroline. I would have no reason in the world to speak to him. When I visited my sister at home, I always made it a point to leave before he got home." Tracy was back in control now.

"Okay, where were you on Wednesday night?" Donna was wrapping this one up.

"I had eaten dinner at Great Wall in Twin Lakes Shopping Center at about six. I guess something didn't agree with me, and I felt ill that night. Nothing terrible, but I stayed in bed all evening and throughout the night," Tracy said as she was deep in thought.

Donna smiled and spoke up. "Oh, I love Great Wall. What did you have?"

Tracy's face lit up. "I had the Roast Pork with Broccoli. You can't beat it for a little over five dollars!" She smiled.

"You got that right! I love their Roast Pork, too." Donna stood to go. "Please stand so I can get a picture of you for the file. Thank you for coming in, Tracy. If you can think of anything that might be of any help, please call."

"One last question." It was Lou this time. "Did you know anything about his business? Where he traveled to? Why he had to travel?"

"No. He seemed very secretive about everything. His business was something Caroline said he never talked about, and he certainly would not tell *me* anything." Tracy picked up her purse to leave and said her goodbyes. Donna had an officer show her out.

Alone in the interview room, Lou and Donna went over their notes. Donna was shocked at the different view of Wilkerson they had with this new information.

"Wanting the kid to be aborted? Do you think he might have thought that it wasn't his? Sounds to me like Caroline met someone who cared more for her than Henry. Maybe Henry had his suspicions or had even found out the truth. That could have been what caused him to kill himself." Lou's attitude had completely changed, and his suspicions were now in full force.

"Whoaaaa there, Red Rover! Back up! We don't have any reason to believe that Caroline had, or has, a boyfriend." Donna was surprised at the force of his convictions.

"Well, I might not have your Mensa IQ, woman, but think about it. What man wants his wife to abort his *own* child? No man in his right mind would do that. Henry must have known it wasn't his. Maybe he was sterile and knew it couldn't be his. Maybe, it was guilt over her own actions that caused her to break down when we told her he might have committed suicide. Maybe, he…."

"Stop right there, Lou. I hear what you're saying, and I'm not dismissing it. I'm just asking that we investigate the possibility with an open mind. We can't go accusing a woman who has just lost her husband without darn good reasons. Right now, we have none.

"I see your point—I do. It could even be motive for her getting rid of her husband." Donna had to acknowledge there may be some truth in this whole new line of thought.

"Not to mention her boyfriend!" Lou gathered his papers and left the room. His day seemed to go down the tubes with this interview.

Donna sat alone for a while and went over everything they'd just learned. Could this be the clue they had overlooked? Caroline was cheating and wanted her husband dead? Could she have had him murdered, or maybe the boyfriend had it done without her knowledge?

They needed to talk with the housekeeper, who was due in for her interview at noon today. If anyone knows what's going on within the walls of a house, it is the hired help.

~~~

Heddy Foster was a stocky, medium-skinned African-American woman. She had short black hair and kind, dark eyes. She appeared to be about 40 and held herself with grace.

Lou got right down to business. "Was Caroline cheating on her husband?"

"Whaaaaaa…!" Heddy's look was not only shock, but anger as well. "Absolutely not! Mrs. Wilkerson is not that type! How DARE you!"

"Of course not," Donna jumped in, giving Lou a glare of her own.

Barely above a whisper, she said to him, "I think that could have been handled a little better."

"Well, I am not talking with him anymore. Either he leaves, or I do." Heddy was fit to be tied.

"Fine." Lou got up and left the room.

After a moment of silence, Donna tried to pick up the pieces.

"I apologize for my partner. He is not having a good day. As for the Wilkerson's' marriage, what can you tell me?"

Heddy thought before answering. "Mr. Wilkerson was a bad man. Really. He was mean to his wife. Mentally mean. I never saw anything physical, but you would have to ask Caroline…uh, Mrs. Wilkerson, about that. He hated kids—I can tell you that!"

"Were you employed by the Wilkersons when Caroline was pregnant?"

"I surely was. She was just radiant and so happy. Now the Mister, that's a different story. He didn't want her to have a kid. He told her to get rid of it. 'Course, a fine lady like Mrs. Wilkerson would never do anything like that."

Donna wanted to know more about his attitude. "Did he change after the baby was born? Many do, after they actually hold their own child."

"Not a chance! If the Missus carried the baby into a room he was in, the man would get up and leave. He never held that child and never spoke her name. After that poor thing died, he acted like she'd never existed." Heddy shook her head at the terrible memory.

Shocked at this new information about the baby's death, Donna asked, "How did the baby die?"

"Crib death. At least that is what they said. That means they really don't know what killed her. They call everything 'crib death' if there ain't any other explanation. Lord knows, she was healthy and well taken care of. Caroline would have starved herself before letting that child go without anything."

"But she *has* a three-year-old child. A girl!" Donna's learning about the death of Caroline's baby wasn't fitting together.

"Adopted." Heddy didn't offer any further explanation. Donna stared at her for a moment then moved on.

"Do you know anything about Mr. Wilkerson's business?"

"No. I don't think anyone did. He wasn't the kind to share his life with anyone. Really secretive, he was. All I know is he traveled a lot. He would call me when he was leaving town so I wouldn't cook his evening meal."

"He called *you* with this information, not Caroline?" Donna couldn't remember if Caroline mentioned who he called.

"Why, of course. He never spoke to Caroline. Their marriage was only for appearances. In the house, they didn't speak to each other, didn't eat with each other, and slept in separate rooms." Heddy didn't mind sharing this information because Caroline told her to be truthful. She certainly didn't want to do anything to harm her dear friend. Caroline meant a lot to her.

67

"Where were you last Wednesday night?" Donna was asking the obvious.

"I got home about seven-thirty that night. My kids were home and had already fixed their own dinner, so we watched a movie on DVD. It was *Frozen*. Again. My kids love it, and I have to admit I do, too. I went to bed at about eleven."

"Do you attend the same church that Caroline does?"

"No, I don't. We're Catholic." Heddy was smiling now at the questions.

Donna returned her smile. "Can you think of anyone who would want to hurt Mr. Wilkerson?"

"I don't personally know of any, but I am sure there are many out there!" Heddy laughed out loud this time.

"One final question." Donna was smiling at the lady across the table. "Do you think Mr. Wilkerson killed himself?"

"Him? The Good Lord knows that man was so arrogant and wrapped up in himself that he would have never harmed a hair on his own perfect head. Not in a million years!" Now both laughed at her answer.

"Thank you for coming in. You've been very helpful." Donna liked this lady.

"My pleasure. And you can tell your partner for me that Caroline is one of the most upstanding ladies I have ever met. She would never go outside her marriage vows, although I would have *loved* to see her do it. *Anything* to get away from that horrible man. But I guess she doesn't have to worry about him any longer."

Donna walked Heddy out. When she returned, Lou was sitting at his desk looking sheepish.

"Can you tell me what *that* was all about? What is *with* you today?" Donna was irritated at his lousy attitude.

"Look, I'm sorry. I'm just not in a very great frame of mind today. I shouldn't have taken it out on the lady, but…."

"No, you *shouldn't* have taken it out on her. And there are no 'buts!' You are supposed to be more professional than that."

Donna stopped, took a deep breath, and then continued, "Okay, let's move on. Heddy only supported what we already knew or suspected. He was one lousy husband, and she also doesn't think he killed himself."

She slapped the file folder down on her desk, not trying to hide the frustration she felt.

CHAPTER

6

By two on Friday afternoon, they received the report from ballistics. The gun was clean—not involved in any other crime they could find.

The serial number had been ground off, and the silencer was not registered, which made it illegal. At this point there was little to lead them to the owner, or the user, of this weapon.

The only prints found were Henry's except for a small smudge on the bottom of the barrel, which may or may not have been his. Nothing could be determined from that. Could this man really have killed himself? Despite their own feelings on the matter, they couldn't rule anything out, yet.

Henry's car was another story. They'd found two more firearms, and one was registered to Henry. There was a large amount of burglary tools in the trunk and a suitcase with clothes and money. Wilkerson's were the only prints found on any of those items. Lou and Donna were stunned to read the report. What was this man into that he needed burglary tools and guns?

They left the precinct for some fresh air. The day was gorgeous, around 70 degrees. The sun cast lazy shadows under the eaves and trees while the breeze made Donna want to curl up on a bench and take a nap. She sighed for no other reason than soaking it all in.

They grabbed a hot-dog and lemonade at the corner stand. Derry's Dogs was always there in good weather. You expected him to be open.

Another month and he would shut down for the winter. Once it got cold, people just didn't walk down the street for a hot-dog

Sitting on a bench, both were quiet for a few moments, eating and thinking.

Why would someone kill another and leave their gun behind?

Killers rarely leave their weapons behind, especially one with an expensive silencer, unless maybe it had been a mistake.

Could it have been suicide? If so, why remove the serial number from the gun? After you pull the trigger, it's not like you're gonna care if anyone knows it's yours.

Or was it something he had used to commit other crimes? Was being a criminal what he did for a living? He was starting to sound like the kind of creep who would do just about anything.

It was legal to own a silencer in most

states, including Kansas, so that was not an issue. But for it to be legal, it had to be registered to the owner. This one was not and, therefore, illegal.

A couple of years ago, the FBI would have gotten involved over the silencer alone. Donna and Lou saw nothing wrong with law-abiding citizens being able to own the same weapons and accessories that were so openly available to criminals.

Strict gun laws would cause crime to skyrocket. Every law-enforcement officer knew that. Why was it so hard for politicians to figure out? Crooks would know honest people wouldn't have any way to defend themselves, so there would be nothing to stop them from robbing and killing. Everyone knows a crook can get any kind of gun he wants, when he wants. Always has and always will.

Dr. K had said there was no sign of a struggle. Another reason to think suicide. People don't normally stand still and let you blow their brains out. And then there was the fact only his prints were on the gun. Could it really be?

"Girl, have you heard when the background report will come in on this guy?" Lou never liked this part of the investigation. All questions and no answers. It was a whole lot more interesting when things started making sense. Now, all they had was a body and a gun. In a church. Period.

"Nope. Tomorrow's Saturday, so I doubt we will see it before Monday. And, it will be another week before all the toxicology reports come in." Donna relished the last bite of her hot-dog and washed it down with the last of her lemonade. Lou may have had breakfast, but she hadn't. She felt better now.

She was looking forward to having the weekend off. Detectives were required to work every other Saturday and one Sunday a month, but this weekend was all hers. She planned to clean house and sleep! But this case would require some of their weekend attention.

"I think we had better show up at that church on Sunday. If it wasn't suicide, our perp may be there." Donna was mostly thinking out loud.

"You mean go to the services in the morning? The actual *church* services?" This is not something Lou considered as a good way to spend his day off.

Donna nudged him and smiled, "You'll survive. I'll even drive."

"You're hard on me, woman," Lou groaned at the thought.

"Say partner, think you will have some time tomorrow to get together? I have something I would like to talk to you about. I mean, if you have time. I know I owe you some explanation…, " Lou looked uncomfortable.

"You don't owe me anything, Lou. I don't know what is going on with you lately that you would be so out of character. You *are* wound a little tight. But, yes, let's have lunch tomorrow. Sounds great, as long as we don't talk about business!" They made plans and then went back to work.

Returning to their office, they stared at the stack of folders that had been dropped on their desks. The initial reports were in on the members of the church. It looked like a lot of reading was in order. Donna and Lou exchanged a look of dread. Most good detectives hate paperwork. Just a fact.

The next few hours would be nothing more than boring tidbits. But those files might contain information they needed to know. Donna grabbed a pile and dumped them on Lou's desk; then she sat down to get started herself. They eliminated the ones they had already spoken with and made notes on the rest.

- Celia Lynette Hess, twenty-nine, single African-American woman, five children under ten years old. Cynthia, nine; Georgia and Galena, twin girls at five; and at three years old the last two were twin boys—Barry and Brady. Works nights at QuickTrip on South Seneca; her neighbor watches the children. Welfare assistance. A breast-cancer survivor. No known ties to the Vic except attending the same church. *Not someone to consider at this time.*

- Hawk Benton, fifty-three years old, recovered addict/alcoholic. Stats showed five-foot-eleven, 240 pounds. He had dropped out of high school in Woodward, Oklahoma, and run away from home at fifteen. Drifter until he came to Wichita. Has done time for fighting. Bad temper. Did a month of county time three years ago; off probation now. No further trouble. *Not in the league of someone who would know Henry, but due to his past, will set this guy aside as someone to look into further.*

- Joe Garrett, forty-two, contract maintenance company, Garrett Enterprises. Boyish good looks, blue eyes. Well thought of, a hard worker. Divorced, one child who had died at birth. Bit of a loner. Is under contract to the Wilkersons to clean windows and maintenance as needed. *Okay, at least Joe knew them. Set him aside for further checking.*

- Margaret and James Casterman, sixties, marriage in crisis. Don't show up to church much anymore. Pastor Tim doesn't know if they are still together or not. *An unhappy couple in their sixties…not what we are looking for.*

- Raychel Garcia, forty-five, female, twice divorced, no children. Fluent in Spanish, English, and German. Senior Stylist at Destiny's Divas, a hair salon in East Wichita. Owns condo on East Harry St. Stylist to Caroline Wilkerson. Attends the same church. *Set aside for now. May want to talk to her.*

- Tracy Lynn Andrews, Caroline Wilkerson's sister, thirty-five. Moved here about five years ago. A writer with several best sellers to her name. Went to same church off and on. *Already interviewed. Set aside to check out her*

79

books!

- Stella Douglas, nineteen, dating Gabe Stanton. Raised by grandmother, now deceased. Inherited small home. Works part time for Lily Stanton and goes to WSU. *Good for her. But we will still need to talk to her.*

By seven o'clock, they both were tired of reading but had managed to comb through several dozen files. With little sleep the night before, Donna mentioned calling it a day and getting a fresh start Monday. Lou was all for it.

With all of the double shifts this past week, they were ready for the weekend off. Donna left while he flipped through a couple more files and then stacked them all back up.

~~~

Donna felt on top of the world when she awoke at eleven on Saturday morning. She was actually able to get twelve hours sleep, and, boy, did she need it! After her shower and applying makeup, she picked out her favorite jeans, boots, and sweatshirt to wear to the arranged lunch date with Lou.

She was looking forward to lunch. Being able to chat with Lou about something besides work would be nice. She liked being friends with her partner, but it wasn't often they could spend off-time together.

Donna headed for the restaurant and thought she saw a pickup truck following her, but she couldn't be sure. It sure seemed like it, though. Changed lanes when she did… all that stuff. But when she pulled into the restaurant parking lot, the truck drove on. It was easy to be wrong about these things.

At one o'clock, she walked into the Texas Roadhouse Restaurant on East Kellogg for her meeting with Lou, and he was waiting for her inside the front door.

"You look positively Texan, girl!" He grinned at her jeans and boots.

"Well *you* don't look any different, Dapper Dan. Don't you ever tire of looking perfect in expensive suits?" Donna teased back.

"You think I look perfect? Why, you flirty cowgirl! Nope, I never do get tired of dressing up! One only dresses 'down' when they mow the lawn, and I pay to have that done, so I never need to look bad." Lou was smiling ear to ear, showing off a perfect smile. It was true—he loved dressing well, which translated as classy and expensive.

"Come on. I already have our table."

Lou sat on the right side of Donna instead of across, so he wouldn't have to yell to be heard. The place was always fun, but on a Saturday afternoon, it was particularly noisy with everyone having a good time.

After ordering, they enjoyed the country music and great food while laughing as the waitresses would break into a line dance to the music while still carrying a tray of steaks. They were not in any hurry to leave.

After lunch, they sipped on sweet tea. Some of the crowd had dissipated, and the place wasn't as noisy.

"So what's on your mind, my friend?" Donna was being gentle about it.

"Well, thanks for taking the time. I have a situation, and would appreciate your opinion on it. You know I value your opinion. And my mother does, too… and…," Lou was stumbling on every word.

"Spit it out, already!" Donna said with a big grin.

"Uh, my girlfriend says she's pregnant."

"Wow." Donna was stopped cold by this unexpcctcd information. "Well… uh… I guess congratulations are in order."

"Well, not exactly. At least not yet…."

83

Lou was struggling to find the right words. "Clarissa wants us to get married right *now*, and I just don't think that's necessary. She's pushing me, and I have been ignoring the subject. But now, with a baby and all, I think I should do the right thing, don't you?"

"What do *you* want to do, Lou?" Donna was becoming concerned for her unhappy friend.

"I don't know. I told my mother…."

"And how is that wonderful woman?" Donna jumped at the chance to talk about his mother. She met Darlene McGregor on a couple of occasions and admired the sweet lady. She was smart as a whip, too! It was obvious where Lou got his intelligence.

Lou had told her the story of his unusual upbringing with his mother. Admiration was what that woman deserved, and Donna was happy to have her as a friend.

"Oh, she's great. Always asks about you. You guys are two peas in a pod, I swear. Anyway, Mom said to make sure it is *my* kid before getting married. You know—wait until it's born and get a DNA test done. I told her I would, but I'm wondering if there is any reason for waiting. I mean, why would I think it's *not* mine?" Lou was looking more unhappy by the minute.

"Wait a minute! Is this the reason you went off about Caroline and Henry's baby? Do you think Clarissa's baby is not yours?"

"No, I mean yes…I mean…," Lou looked sheepish.

"What I mean is, yes, I think the baby is mine. Why wouldn't it be? And yes, I might have overreacted to the Wilkerson information. I have been a bit on edge over this whole thing."

"A *bit* on edge! Seriously? How about 'fell *off* the edge?' Donna teased and then went on. "Well, at least I can see what started it all."

"Yeah, I'm sorry. I know I was wrong. My emotions took over when I shouldn't have let them."

"Okay, let's get back to your problem. How is your relationship with Clarissa? Do you guys get along and all?" Donna was picking up on something that just wasn't right, and she wanted to find out why.

"Not really. We fight all the time. She is insanely jealous of you—I've told you that. She goes crazy to think I spend more time with you than with her." Lou added with a lecherous grin, "I guess I would, too, if I was her."

"Cute, Lou." Donna's cheeks felt a little warm, so she quickly moved on, "The first time I met Clarissa was at her own mother's house for a Bar-B-Q, remember? I can't say I was too impressed with her then. Oh, I don't mean there is anything wrong with her, just that she treated her mother like she was hired help or something."

Donna didn't want to come across as not liking Clarissa, even though that much was true. After all, Lou might marry this woman! The fact that she didn't like her would have to be kept secret. Whenever Donna was around, Clarissa started an argument of some kind with Lou and ruin the day for everyone. She could just imagine how bad it got when they were alone!

"I know, always giving orders. She looks down on everyone else. I think the thing that bothers me the most is how she clings to me like I'm her lifeline. I don't like it, and I have told her. She says she loves me so much she can't bear to have me out of her sight." Lou was staring at the floor by his feet.

"Okay, you want my advice? Here it is. Do what your mother asked of you. You already promised her and you have to keep your word, Lou. But it's a smart decision.

"Wait until the baby is born. Have the DNA test. Then, if it is yours, you can decide what you want to do. *Now* is not the time for you to make life-changing decisions—you are too emotional about it at this point.

"When the baby is born, and if the child is yours, then you can decide if you want to spend the rest of your life with Clarissa or not. You don't have to be married to the mother to be a good father. But that would have to be your decision at that time. Just put it one foot in front of the other. You don't have to win the race today." Donna was very sincere in her opinion, whether Lou liked it or not.

"You're right. I promised my mother I would wait. I guess that is the best solution. Thanks for hearing me out. Believe it or not, I consider you a good friend, and your opinion means a lot. Lunch is on me!" Lou grabbed the ticket before Donna could and called the waitress over.

"You had *better* consider me a friend. I am the one who has your back.... or *not*... you know, depending on how I feel that day...," Donna looked disinterested. They shared the same sense of humor.

"Oh, that's just fine, Mr. Scrooge. Don't expect Jacob Marley to come running to *your* rescue, either!" Lou pretended to be put off.

In the parking lot, Donna gave him a hug and told him she knew he would do the right thing about Clarissa and the baby. All he needed to do was trust his own instincts.

Lou asked what she would be doing the rest of the day. After thinking a moment, Donna said, "I will get the house cleaned up, and then I think I will go to Great Wall for dinner. For some reason, I want good Chinese."

Before saying goodbye, she reminded him she would be at his home at 9 AM the next morning—for church!

"You will be the death of me, woman!" Lou laughed as he got into his Mercedes and drove away.

MURDER FOR A MOMENT

CHAPTER

7

After lunch with Lou, Donna spent the afternoon cleaning her place and doing laundry. Her mind was never far from Lou's situation. She cared about her friend and didn't want anyone to take advantage of him. On a personal level, he was sweet and kind, just like his mother. He was too trusting of other people. At least that was her opinion.

She couldn't shake his situation from her

mind. Lou's story played out in her thoughts.

Lou's background was amazing. He'd come from mixed parentage. Lou's mother, a beautiful, light-skinned African-American woman by the name of Darlene Loretta Feldman fell deeply in love with a white boy, Sebastian Christian McGregor. He felt the same about her and they eloped, much to the horror of his family.

Sebastian was the son of a very wealthy and prominent white Wichita family who owned several high-end car dealerships under the corporate name of McGregor Motor Corp.

As she loaded the dishwasher, Donna thought about the problems mixed marriages would have caused back in the late-seventies. They were not as accepted then as they are today.

But being prominent Christians in the community, the McGregor family put on a front of acceptance. *Whether they did approve or not, Sebastian and Darlene were legally married.*

The kitchen was spotless, so stripping the bed and finishing the laundry were next on Donna's list.

In the fourth year marriage, Darlene gave birth to Lou. His father was already withdrawing his affections somewhat from Darlene. Lou said his mother protected him from any feelings of neglect by telling him his father had to work long hours.

The dryer buzzer went off, and Donna went to hang clothes while they were still warm. But first, into the washer went the bedding.

Just after the McGregor's' sixth anniversary, when Lou was only two years old, Sebastian ran off with a very wealthy white woman who lived in Kansas City, Missouri. His family was behind him 100% but feared what it would cost the family in money to get rid of Darlene and her unwanted black child.

Donna could only wonder what had gone through their minds during that time, but it made her smile. *Hypocrites.*

Being the intelligent woman she was, Darlene had her attorney draw up the most amazing divorce agreement. She agreed not to ask for any alimony or child support for their son on two conditions.

First, Sebastian was to pay all of her attorney fees regarding his divorce, and any other case that may come out of this divorce.

Second, he would have to state for the court that the other woman wooed him away and captured his heart, thus causing him to end their marriage.

Sebastian and his attorney apparently thought they had hit the jackpot. Darlene could have asked for a lot of money, so this agreement was better than anything they ever thought possible. Just pay her attorney and never have to pay alimony or child support? You have got to be kidding! All he had to do was admit to his adultery! Sebastian quickly signed the deal, and his family was ecstatic to hear about it.

Donna had now finished the laundry, and it was time to vacuum the floors. As she pulled out the vacuum and plugged it in, she recalled what Lou had told her about the divorce.

Appearing in court for their divorce, as agreed, Sebastian stood up and told all about his affair and leaving his wife for a rich, beautiful, and sexy woman. The woman was in court to back him up, and smiled at him as he told of their wonderful love for each other. He enjoyed recalling all of their clever plans while exchanging looks with his paramour.

The judge apparently was not too keen on the agreement leaving the wife with no income. He asked Darlene if she had agreed to this. She did. He asked if she'd been coerced into it or threatened in any way. She hadn't. She explained to the judge it was her idea and she was comfortable with it.

He stated to the court he didn't like divorces that required no child support from the father, but he would accept the wife's request. But in doing so, the judge removed any parental rights to the child's father. Sebastian had no problem with that, either.

After the judge granted the divorce, Sebastian and his future bride quickly disappeared to get started on their celebration. Darlene and her attorney, however, took their time. On their way out, they stopped long enough to file a lawsuit.

The "Alienation of Affections" lawsuit was not against Sebastian, but the mistress, even though Sebastian would have to pay all of the attorney's fees. Not every state had this option, but Kansas did. There was no denying the charges because of the testimony in court records, by the husband, as to the "cause" of leaving his wife.

The defendant knew she didn't have a prayer, so, within a year, an out-of-court settlement had been reached for $2.5 million. This sum was many times more than the amount Darlene could ever have gotten in alimony or child support combined.

Donna never tired of thinking about the whole story. What a smart lady Darlene was!

From what Lou told her, Darlene set aside half a million for him that tripled in size by the time he went off to college, and she invested the rest to ensure that she would never need to worry about money again.

Another reason to admire the woman was that Donna knew both Lou and Darlene lived in Woodlawn Village, a nice upper-middle-class area to be sure, but they could have afforded much better.

Putting on airs was not who Darlene and Lou were. They only lived three blocks apart. Darlene's sprawling ranch on North Rutland Street had a pool, but Lou's house on North Stratford didn't. Darlene used the pool to get him to come over more often, and it usually worked.

Donna had even gone over to Darlene's home one day and enjoyed a leisurely afternoon around the pool. That is until Lou and Clarissa got into it about why Donna was there, too. Clarissa made it clear about not wanting his "other" woman around when she was. Donna got out of the lounger and quietly left, winking at Darlene on her way out.

As for the Missouri lovers, Lou showed her the newspaper clippings how Sebastian had been killed two years after the settlement. Seems he was driving drunk, went off the road, and hit a cement barrier.

Not one to carry a grudge, Darlene sent flowers to his funeral. She also kept the newspaper articles for when Lou was old enough to understand. He said his mother rarely dated as he was growing up. She had loved Sebastian with all her heart and didn't seem to want to find a replacement.

Donna felt that was a choice each person had to make for themselves and could hardly fault Darlene.

So, Lou's Mercedes and fifteen hundred-dollar suits were certainly accounted for. Without knowing his background, one would think he was a cop on the take. *He does love dressing well.*

Donna laughed out loud at her last thought. Her partner in pinstriped three-piece suits, and she, the original jeans and high heel boots girl! Sure she could dress up when she had to, but her dress of choice was comfy jeans. Her favorite color of jeans was actually black, but she had all colors. They made a strange team, but somehow, it worked out better than either one of them could have imagined.

Once again, she felt she needed to agree with Darlene about this current situation. *Waiting to ensure that the baby was Lou's really was the right decision. Marriage is a major step and shouldn't be taken lightly.*

The housecleaning was all done, so after a quick shower and clean clothes, Donna headed for the Great Wall and some good food.

Getting home a couple of hours later, she cuddled up on the couch to watch her favorite DVD for the umpteenth time, *The Lion King*. Then it was time to get some sleep.

Her last waking thought was hoping Lou

would listen to his mother….

CHAPTER

8

Sunday morning was classic "autumn in Kansas." A soft breeze whispered to colorful, dancing leaves while the sun dictated the brilliance of the day.

Donna left her condo early for a chance to enjoy the wonderful day, not often found in the Plains states. Fall in Kansas can be beautiful one moment and buried in a snow storm the next—or worse, flattened by a killer tornado. Tornadoes were rare in the fall but not unheard of. But for now, she would enjoy this picture-perfect morning.

Grabbing coffee and a breakfast burrito at a fast-food joint, she headed for the park, not far from Lou's place. When she sat down at a picnic table, she called Lou's cell.

"This is your conscience calling. It is time to get out of bed and hit the shower. God is expecting you at 'His' house this morning!" Donna knew it would be at least an hour before he forgave her.

"Very funny. It's just like you to take pleasure in ruining a man's day off." Lou had been sound asleep.

"You have one half-hour to become human. I will be outside your place at nine-thirty to pick you up. Church starts at ten. If you are not outside, ready to leave, I will lay on the horn—awakening all your neighbors!" She hung up before he could yell back at her. She chuckled as she unwrapped her burrito and bit down.

Donna went over in her mind the church members they had only read about. All they had seen were DMV photos, so it would be interesting to see how well they could pick out each member dressed in their Sunday best. Current photos had been taken of the ones they were able to interview.

Just so she wouldn't jump out at everyone as not belonging there, she dressed in a medium-blue pant suit, ivory blouse, and heels. The outfit made her blue eyes jump out like sapphires.

On time, Donna pulled into his driveway. Standing outside, Lou slid into the passenger side of her car. His wolf whistle was sincere.

"You show up for work looking like that, girl, and none of those beat boys will ever get anything done! You look positively *illegal* this morning."

Lou knew she was beautiful, but every time he'd laid eyes on her, it was like he had to remind himself all over again how stunning she was. The incredible thing was she didn't seem to be aware of how her looks affected people. That nonchalance about her looks only made her seem more beautiful, if that was possible.

Lou, himself, sported a dark gray pinstriped suit, white shirt, and burgundy tie. Dressed to the teeth, as always.

Donna ignored his reference to her looks and said, "You look pretty good yourself, even though I had to threaten you. See, going to church can be a benefit. You get to wear your new suit for all to see!"

"Yeah, yeah. Drive, nagging person. You owe me a good lunch after getting me up so early, and you're paying this time."

"Ha! I doubt Clarissa would like knowing you were having lunch with me on a Sunday afternoon and not her! Let alone lunch together for two days in a row."

"You're right about that. She had a cow when she found out about my working with you today," Lou offered, "but she'll get over it."

She pulled onto Kellogg, also known as

Highway fifty-four, going west from Lou's place. There it was again—that pickup truck. Was it the same one? It had to be following her, but why? She could tell there was a single driver, a male, behind the wheel. She said nothing to Lou, but watched her rear view mirror as they headed toward the church. It *was* following her, right?

Upon arriving at the church, the news about Henry's death had its effect. The parking lot was full, and cars were parking on the street. This small church was going to be full today.

She drove further to turn around for a parking place, but the truck she thought was following her pulled into the lot. Donna felt like a fool. The darn truck wasn't following *her;* it was going to the same place! *Get a grip, girl!*

After driving the extra block, she turned around and could park by the curb about a half-block away. She could see people walking into the church. Donna picked up her camera and took pictures of people milling around outside and opening the door for others to enter. It never hurt to have something to look at later to help remember.

"I thought of the same thing," Lou said as he touched his upper left jacket pocket.

"Thought of what?" Then she saw it. Lou was wearing his pocket camera, not much bigger than a credit card. It was poised to take pictures through the pocket button hole.

"As soon as I turn it on, it will take a picture every 30 seconds. Only one megabyte clarity, but it's good for three hours." Lou touched a little lever and the first picture of the windshield was taken.

"Brilliant, as usual. Let's get in there." Donna exited the car, with Lou right behind her.

As expected, someone was at the door to welcome them. As they entered, Lou whispered, "It will be full, so you go to the right, and I'll head left." With that, they split, to appear to be separate from each other.

As with any church, just before services

started, everyone was talking and greeting each other. Donna walked in front of the back pew until she was again on the parking-lot-side aisle. She leaned against the wall and just watched the commotion, taking in the people, conversations, and anything else that might help.

People came up to her, introduced themselves, and welcomed her.

"I don't think I've seen you before. My name is Raychel. Welcome. We hope you will come back again."

Raychel. Donna remembered she was Caroline Wilkerson's hair dresser. The woman just seemed to glow. Mid-forties, divorced, and a fanatic for the Lord. Just goes to show you: You don't have to be young to have the light of the Holy Spirit with you.

"Thank you," Donna answered as Raychel moved on to greet others. She recognized some of the others from their pictures. Seeing Pastor Stanton walk up onto the stage and set his briefcase down, she moved up the side aisle until she could get his attention. He stepped off the stage next to her.

Bending his head down, Donna whispered into his ear, "My partner and I are here today. Please do not point that out to everyone. We are here to observe."

Pastor Tim didn't say anything; he nodded and went back to the stage. Music started, and people were settling down. Donna went to the back of the church and stood against the wall to watch. Lou was doing the same thing on the other side.

The church was not full but almost. It gave Donna a homey feeling. Yes, it was small, but that by itself was inviting. Everyone seemed to know everyone else here.

Not quite like the church I go to. People don't know who is sitting next to them, with what, maybe 1,000 members? I'll bet it feels good coming here, she thought. *They are building a new sanctuary, and you know there will be some of these people who will hate to leave this building.*

She looked around and didn't see Caroline Wilkerson in attendance. Donna didn't blame her, with all she was going through. She glanced at Lou, who winked back and continued watching the crowd.

She picked up on Lily and her son, Gabe. Stella was sitting next to him. Joe Garrett was in attendance, as were both Walker families. They were on stage getting ready to play and sing.

Donna made notes on others she was pretty sure of, but wanted to check with the files.

The music stopped, and Pastor Tim went to the podium.

MURDER FOR A MOMENT

CHAPTER

9

Monday morning found Donna waiting for Hawk Benton to show up for his interview, while buried in a ton of paperwork. Lou hadn't made it in, either.

Yesterday's church services had gone well, although neither one of them could detect anything out of the ordinary among the parishioners. She hadn't had time to go through all of the photos but expected no surprises. She remembered seeing Benton there, however.

After church, they'd gone to lunch again. After agreeing that neither one had seen anything out of the ordinary, they sat back and had a great time joking and laughing about life in general.

"So, what do you want out of life, Donna?" Lou had asked.

Instead of coming back with a jab, she decided to speak the truth.

"I guess I want the same thing everyone else wants, Lou—to be loved. All humans want that. It's innate in us. Living only for yourself is not very fulfilling." That's how she felt, and Lou was a close-enough friend to confide in.

Lou was quiet for a moment as the seriousness of her answer caught him off guard.

"I never thought of it that way, girl, but you're right. No matter what material things you might have or want—a bigger house, a certain car, or anything, it doesn't replace that desire to be loved. Hmm, you are pretty smart for a little girl." Lou couldn't resist a little jab, but it only got him a kick in the shins under the table. "OW!"

"What happened, Lou, did your ego get hurt?" Donna was now having fun.

Now the weekend was over, and it was back to work. Hawk was due in at nine o'clock, so she had about ten minutes to go over his file when Lou came in.

"Nice of you to show up, even if you are late. Hot date last night?" Donna tried to keep it light because the look on Lou's face did not bode well.

"She left me." Lou got right to the point.

"What? Who?" She couldn't make sense of his statement at first, but he definitely had her attention.

"When I got home, she had packed up her clothes and left. Clarissa left a note she was moving in with her mother until I came to my senses and wanted to marry the woman having his child." Lou seemed miserable and confused.

He continued, "Yesterday morning, just before you picked me up at nine-thirty, I told Clarissa I was having lunch with you again to go over some things about the case.

"She said if I walked out that door and left with you, she would be gone when I came back. She was not going to stand for me spending my off time with you. I didn't think she meant it because she is always saying dumb stuff about you, but I guess she did."

Lou sat on his chair with his elbows on his knees while he stared at the floor.

After several moments of silence, Donna walked over to him and put a hand on his shoulder.

"Lou, she's just upset, but she will calm down. She always does. Give it a week or two. In the meantime, leave her alone. She needs the time to figure things out for herself, and so do you. It'll be all right—you'll see. Just be patient."

Lou looked up at her standing next to his chair and sighed. "You're right. I know you are. I don't like it, but I'll behave and give her some space." He took another deep breath and saw Hawk Benton walk through the door.

"You want to take this one, or do you want me to?" He was now looking at his partner.

"Why don't we both listen to what he has to say, unless you would like to dive into this paperwork?" Donna knew what his answer would be.

They both escorted him to the interview room and spent the next hour learning more about this man.

Lou started out with, "Did you know the deceased?"

"Ycs."

"Ever see him outside of church?"

"No."

"What did you think of him?"

"He was a weasel." Benton stared at the floor, not looking at either one.

"Weasel?" It was Donna this time.

"That's as nice as I can put it." Hawk was obviously trying to hold back emotions.

"Why do you think he was a 'weasel,' Mr. Benton?"

"Call me 'Hawk.' No one calls me 'Mr. Benton.' I'm not the only one who felt that way. He just was. He was a phony, always bragging about his life and all he had."

Lou looked at Donna. Was this man jealous of all that Wilkerson had, or did it go deeper? She raised an eyebrow letting him know she felt the same way.

"Did you resent what he had?"

"Are you *LISTENING?* I don't give a…. I don't *care* about what he owned. He was just a rotten person—that's it." Hawk was red-faced and nervous. He kept his head down.

"Okay. Got it." It was Donna's turn. "What made him a rotten person?"

"What didn't, would be an easier question to answer. He came across as so holier-than-thou with all of his business interests and his beautiful wife. Never wanting her to talk to anyone else. Not even a woman!

"She was standing in the aisle after service one Sunday. A pretty young brunette came up to her and was trying desperately to talk to her. Man, that creep appeared out of nowhere and grabbed his wife's arm and drug her out, leaving that poor woman just standing there, shocked and mad. She sure was pissed off.

"Mrs. Wilkerson is a sweet lady. Really nice, especially when he wasn't around. And real pretty, she is. Can't imagine why he would want to cheat on her! Some men are just never satisfied with what they have."

117

Now he had the undivided attention of both detectives. Lou jumped on this information.

"What makes you think he cheated on her, Mr… uh... Hawk?"

"Oh, *please!* The man had 'porn' tattooed on each eyeball. Not a woman walked by that he didn't check out every portion of her. I caught him…." Hawk stopped suddenly and refused to go on.

"You caught him doing what, Hawk?"

"Nothing. Just nothing. Can I go now, or am I gonna get blamed for killing the guy?" Hawk couldn't wait to get out of there. He had had his share of police stations in his day.

Donna had to ask, "*Did* you kill him, Hawk?"

Hawk's shoulders slumped, and he sighed. Finally looking Donna in the eye, he said, "I wanted to, Detective. The Good Lord knows my heart, and I wanted to. But I didn't. That's the truth—take it or leave it."

Lou stood and said, "You can go, Hawk. Thank you for coming in. We may have more questions later, so…"

"…don't leave town. I know. Boy, do I *know*." With a frown, Hawk Benton hurried out of the last place he wanted to be.

~~~

Lou and Donna sat back down in the interview room and just stared at each other for a moment. Cheating? That opened up a different Pandora's Box.

Donna started, "So, what do you think? Did the wife know and kill him in a fit of anger? Did he mess with the wrong wife and some angry husband did him in? Maybe she was underage, and someone killed him for being a pedophile?"

"All of the above. Crap, girl, we have a

huge quandary here all of a sudden. You have to admit, this really opens a can of worms. We need to talk again with all of the women and see if he had ever…well, you get my drift."

"Yeah. We have to start over." Donna's frustration showed.

CHAPTER

10

"That Douglas girl still coming in this afternoon?" Lou was trying very hard to avoid more paperwork.

"Yes, after Angela Preston, the web designer, and Joe Garrett. In the meantime, whether we like it or not, it is back to the paperwork."

"No doubt about it, Slave-Driver Woman:

You are out to kill me. I just know it."

"When did *you* get so smart?" Donna ducked as an eraser came flying her direction.

~~~

"Mr. Wilkerson? I am afraid he was a man who made women nervous. Whether he did it on purpose, I don't know. When I came across him before or after the services, I didn't like the way he looked at me. Stupid, I know," Angela Preston added this bit when she came in for her interview.

"In what way do you mean, exactly?" Donna wanted to know.

"Well, he just undressed women with his eyes. I am an overweight grandmother and he even gave *me* the creeps! Look, Detective, as beautiful as you are, I am sure you have run into a lot of men like that." Angela had a big smile on her face.

Donna's cheeks turned red, so Lou jumped in, unable to miss the chance to rib his partner. "We know what you mean, Angela. Detective Decker gets that all the time! Gets undressed by men wherever she goes!"

"HEY!" Donna glared at Lou and then smiled.

All three were laughing when Lou continued, "Did you ever see him actually try to hit on any woman at the church?"

"No, I… well, there was this one conversation I heard of that didn't seem to go well. He walked up to the front and started a conversation with Stella. She…"

"Stella who?" Donna was making notes even though the recorder was on. She knew who Stella was, but wanted to make sure there wasn't another one around.

"Stella Douglas. She's Gabe Stanton's girlfriend. A real sweetheart, and everyone loves her. Young thing, I think she's eighteen or nineteen. I don't think she has hit twenty yet. Anyway, let me tell you, she looks a whole lot younger than she really is!"

Angela continued, "This one particular day, Wilkerson walked up front and stopped to talk to her. She smiled and was nice to him, but he must have said something wrong because the smile left her face—and I have *never* seen that happen before.

"She stared up at him in shock for a few seconds and then walked away without a word. When Wilkerson turned around, he was smiling this creepy kind of smirk. It gave me goose bumps.

"He saw me looking at him, and he winked at me as he walked back to his wife. Ugh." Angela shuddered thinking about it.

They continued talking with Angela concerning the deceased. She had never seen him outside of church, nor did she know about any of his businesses. Lou and Donna wrapped up the interview, and Angela left.

"Well, I think we can mark her off our 'possible' list," Donna said.

"Yeah, I feel the same way. The only problem I see now is that everyone who ever knew him has just become a suspect." Lou threw the file down on his desk with a loud slap.

"Yeah, and Stella is coming in after Garrett today, so it will be interesting to see what upset her so much." Donna didn't like the road this was taking them down. Back to the paperwork until something interesting turned up.

~~~

Joe Garrett has a contract maintenance company, Garrett Enterprises. Donna interviewed him alone, as Lou was tied up on the phone.

Joe didn't know Wilkerson and couldn't remember him at all. He said he concentrated on

125

the Lord when he was in His house, so there were only a few people he spoke with. And no, he would never give out the building security code. Ever.

"What did you do after church on Wednesday?"

"I went home and then straight to bed." Joe was friendly but a little nervous. He wasn't used to being face to face with a Police Detective. "I had to be up early on Thursday."

"And no one can testify to that fact because you live…" Donna didn't get to finish her statement.

"Yes! I mean, no…. Uh… Yes, I live alone, but my neighbors knew exactly when I get home!" Joe's eyes were big.

"How would your neighbors know when you got home or that you didn't leave again later?"

"I have two German Shepherd mix dogs. Wc are close, you know? They get all excited when I come home and bark loud enough to wake the dead. It bothers my neighbors so I try not to get home late at night, but they know I go to church on Wednesday nights. If I had left later, the ruckus it would have caused when I came home again would have made them really mad." Joe even smiled at that thought. "I guess I never thought that situation would be to my advantage!"

Donna made a quick call to send a uniform to the neighbor's door. A call back within fifteen minutes confirmed the dogs were throwing fits a little after nine Wednesday night when Joe got home. No, there hadn't been any further barking that night.

She thanked Joe for coming in and asked him to let her know if he remembered anything that might be important.

After he left, she wondered if he'd left his house later, what's to say he even came back home in the middle of the night? He could have returned home the next day, when the neighbors wouldn't have cared. She wasn't ready to write him off just yet.

Lou finished with his business call and wanted to be in on the next interview.

~~~

Stella Douglas walked into the precinct at two o'clock, Monday afternoon. She was escorted into the interview room and declined a soda, as she'd brought her own sweet tea with her. She was in good spirits and had a big smile on her face.

Donna was shocked at how right Angela was about Stella's youthful appearance. Though nineteen, the girl could have passed for fourteen or fifteen.

Time to get started, "Hi. Thanks for coming down to talk with us. We just need to clear a couple of things up, if you don't mind."

"Heavens, no! Can't imagine what I can tell you, but it is no trouble at all. I don't have classes today!" Stella was an over-the-top perky kind of girl.

"As you know," Lou said, "a man died in the church last week, and we're talking with those who may have known him. Did you happen to know him?" Both Donna and Lou were watching her face and eyes for any sign of a lie.

"Well, I didn't really know him. He went to our church, of course. I didn't have much to do with him, to tell the truth. The man gave me the willies." The perky slowed down on her face.

"Why is that?" It was Donna who was trying to coax information out of a young girl.

Stella glanced up at Lou and then proceeded slowly, "Well, I never really noticed him. I mean, he wasn't friendly with Gabe and the other people we hang out with, so he never really entered my mind, you know?"

Again, Donna spoke softly to her, "Sure, we know. Why would you have any contact with him? After all, he was twice your age and all…."

"Well, there was this one time, about a

month ago that he came up to me. I was a bit surprised, but sometimes people come up to me thinking I can get something done for them since I am dating Gabe. I don't know why they think that, though. I am just another worshiper of Jesus, like them."

"Can't imagine why they would bother you, but you do have kind of an 'in' with Gabe at your side." Lou was taking a lesson from Donna and spoke softly and supportive. Stella smiled up at him.

Donna was next, acting like a young thing, herself, "Well, what in the world did he want, Stella? Whatever would he be bothering you about?"

"He… he… said…," Stella gulped and took a deep breath. Then she spit it out, "He said men would pay good money to be with a girl like me. That's what he said."

She took another deep breath and continued, "I was so stunned, I just stared at him until the words completely soaked in, and then I turned and walked away. I couldn't think of one thing to say to him. Why would he say such a thing to me?" Now she was about ready to cry.

Donna moved over into the chair next to her and put her arms around her. "Don't give it a second thought, young lady. Some people are just mean. Besides, you know sometimes we get tested, and it is pretty obvious you passed with flying colors!"

Stella perked up with a small smile. "You think so? You really think so? Like God just had him say something awful as a test? Wow. It probably was. Thank you so much for helping me understand!"

Lou jumped in while the girls were still hugging each other. "We know Gabe has the code to the church. Did he ever share that code with you?"

Donna and Stella physically separated, and Stella's smile came bubbling back.

"Good gracious, no! Why in the world would I need the code? Gabe picks me up for church, and he takes me home. *Gabe* is my code, Detective!" Stella looked so proud that she could burst.

"Can you think of any way that Wilkerson could have gotten the code to the church security system?" Donna needed to clear that up.

"Noooo… I can't think of anyone who would want him to go into the church alone. But stop and think about it. Why would he even *want* to be there alone? My goodness, no."

They spent the better part of the next hour talking with her and just getting a feel for what she might know. Sometimes people knew things and were not aware of it.

It was going on four when Lou and Donna thanked her for coming in. Stella got up to leave when she turned and said, "You know, I can't say I really liked the man at all. But I sure wouldn't wish him dead. I can't imagine what happened. It's just terrible. He has been in my prayers since he died."

She then left with the same bubbly personality she came in with.

"We have to recheck with every woman who might have had contact with him." Lou nodded his agreement at Donna's idea.

Returning to their desks, Donna found the autopsy report from Dr. K., sitting on her desk. She glanced through it and then read sections out loud for Lou's benefit.

"Good health, body well taken care of, kidneys, heart and liver healthy, which means the tox report will probably show no long-occurring drug or alcohol use. But we will see if there is any short-term problem.

"Due to the circumstances surrounding the body, it could be a homicide. No sign of a struggle lends credence to suicide. At this time, until new information comes in, I have to rule this death as UNDETERMINED. Signed by Dr. K."

Lou sat down in his chair and said, "Does

that mean…"

"Yep. Square one. Again. We're not getting anywhere… but we're getting there really fast."

CHAPTER

11

Tuesday morning, they made a point of calling all the women on their list, already interviewed or not.

"Well, no," Lily Stanton said. "I don't believe I ever saw him acting improperly to a woman. But remember, I was seldom in his presence."

~~~

"Good gracious, no!" Willy Walker said. "Course I only spoke with him once or twice."

"I admit to feeling a little uncomfortable around him. No reason. Truly, no reason at all. I never saw him act inappropriately to a woman. It's just, well, it's not the way he acted, but the way he looked at women. Like he was evaluating them for some reason.

"Please don't take my thoughts seriously. I'm sure he meant no harm to anyone. I could have imagined it." Jill Walker just didn't know if her feelings were real or not. She certainly didn't want to bad-mouth an innocent person.

~~~

"I have to get out of this chair!" Donna was tired of talking on the phone and getting nowhere.

"I hear ya. It's about eleven-thirty. Let's go to lunch. I've gotta stretch my back a bit. Who's buying lunch this time?" Lou stated.

Donna punched his arm and said it was her treat as she guided him to the door. She drove, not letting him know their destination until they arrived.

"The Great Wall restaurant!" Lou perked up. "I remember you talking about this. Good food, you said."

"You need to get out more, Lou. I know this place is on the west side of town, but really, just because you live on the east side doesn't mean they won't allow you over here." Donna smiled.

After being ushered in, they sat at a table by the window. Their orders were taken and Donna asked if they would leave one menu. Lou thought it odd but said nothing when the request was granted.

After lunch arrived, they became quiet as they inhaled the delicious food.

"How is it?" Donna asked, watching her partner gulping it down.

"It's great. I can't believe I have never eaten here before." Lou had no problem shoveling down what remained on his plate.

"Well, I brought you here for a reason. Remember on Monday, Caroline's sister, Tracy, said she had dinner here at six in the evening?" Donna saw the recognition in Lou's eyes.

"Well, she said she had Roast Pork and Broccoli for a little over five dollars? Check the menu for that information." Donna sat and waited.

Lou grabbed the menu, very curious this time. As he looked through it, his brows knitted in concentration. Slowly, his brows lifted and he said, "Oookaaay. Houston, we have a problem. That price is good only for the lunch specials." The menu showed the special price ends at three-thirty in the afternoon.

"Yep, she didn't eat here Wednesday night; she ate here at lunch on Wednesday. I came out here to eat last Saturday night. I talked with the owner and showed him the picture of Tracy. He recalled her because she was so attractive. Funny what men will remember. Anyway, he said she was not here in the evening.

"Wednesdays are a slow night for them, and he remembered the few locals who came in. Plus, he said he'd never heard of anyone getting sick from his food. Since the same food was served to several people, he is sure he would have known about it had there been a problem." Donna took a breath and stopped talking. She wanted Lou to have time to catch up with all she was saying.

"So she lied to us," he said.

"Looks that way. She wasn't here in the evening, so most likely, she didn't get sick from this food. Now the question is, 'Why would she lie'?" Donna kept tossing ideas around but

139

wanted to hear what Lou thought.

"Why? Well, maybe she didn't lie exactly but forgot what time she came. Maybe she came right at three-thirty and that was actually dinner for her since she wouldn't be hungry later." Lou put himself in her shoes for the moment.

"I thought of that, also. If I ate at around that time, I wouldn't be eating dinner later. But, if she ate that early, then why did she not get ill until seven?" Donna was thinking out loud.

"Obviously she became ill from something else, not the food here." Lou certainly didn't have a problem cleaning his plate.

"True. It could have been something out of her own refrigerator. Not much to go on, but I think she needs to clear up some things."

Donna finished her plate and prepared to leave. More files to go through. The world was full of files, and she was pretty sure they were all sitting on her desk.

It was about one o'clock when they returned. Lou found a new folder on his desk. It turned out to be the information he'd requested on Wilkerson's businesses. It was a day late, but it's what they were waiting for.

Lou sat down and read while Donna went to get them both a soda.

When she returned, she asked, "Well, what have we learned about his business practices? Anything fascinating?"

"Aw, yes, business...," Lou smirked. "What didn't the man do? He invested in high-end swimming pools with a guy in Denver who was later found to be laundering money for the mob. No wrongdoing could be attached to Wilkerson, so he was never charged with a crime. He tripled his money, however, before the business was shut down. We're talking seven figures here!

"Then we go on to a Mercedes dealership in Dallas. He put a sizable amount of money into that, and it seems he tripled it again. That is just before the owner went down for transporting drugs in the door liners of new cars. Another seven-figure profit."

Lou was playing with the papers in his folder. He slapped down the reports about those two places and then picked up another.

"Now we go to Kansas City, MO. It seems that he actually had money invested in some legit businesses; however, the man just couldn't resist a challenge. Last year, a Rupert Begley was busted for running a drug ring. Guess who apparently cashed in on those deals, too?" Lou slapped that report down, too.

"The man puts his money into things that leave the business owner liable if anything goes wrong. But, that is not the worst of it." Lou was shaking his head.

"What could be worse than money laundering and drugs, for heaven sakes, Lou?" Donna threw her hand up dismissively.

"Well, how about rape?"

"*WHAAAAT?*" Donna's mouth dropped open, and her eyes were big. This had come right out of left field. The shock of her exclamation had others around them looking over to see what the problem could be.

"Well, let me back up a step. He was never charged with rape, like he was never charged with any of the other stuff. Seems two women, one in Kansas City and one in Denver, filed a complaint he raped them. Both said they were given a date-rape drug, probably GHB, but there's no way of knowing for sure. Neither could be proved, and he walked again. However, both of them were party girls, and it really was a 'he said, she said' kind of deal."

Lou just stared at the report. It was impossible to figure out the truth when it is just facts in black and white. *Was the man guilty, or did he get a bum rap from two women who were sorry they'd taken him home?*

"What have we got here, Lou? A man who is a crook, cheats on his wife, even stoops to raping those who say 'No?' Why are we even looking for his killer? I would have wanted to do it myself!" Donna was fuming.

"Well, it certainly gives credence to what Benton told us. Maybe he was a philanderer—at best—or a rapist at worst. But it opens a whole new barrel of possibilities.

"We will need to get in touch with Denver and K.C. and get a copy of their files. We will also have to talk to these women. Think one of them might have been so angry they visited Henry in his own hometown?"

"I don't know, but I'm ready to give them a medal if they did." Donna was still fuming. "I'll take Kansas City; you call Denver."

For about an hour, faxes kept pouring in from the other police departments. Putting together the documents, sorting them, and combing through them all for information took time, but Donna and Lou set about their tasks.

"Lou, you get the Denver woman's alibi for last Wednesday night, and I'll do the same with our gal in K.C."

"Don't forget that it could be any of the business owners Henry walked away from and left holding the bag." Lou couldn't count them out.

"Check and see if they are still in lockup. If so, move on. If not, we will have to track *them* down, too."

MURDER FOR A MOMENT

CHAPTER

12

On Wednesday morning, Donna studied the Kansas City, Missouri, file. It seemed a bartender-waitress at a nightclub had filed a report she was drugged and raped by Henry Wilkerson.

Her statement was dated four years previous. Donna read it and couldn't believe what it said:

"It was a slow night at work and toward the end of the evening, Wilkerson was the only one there. I was harassed by a couple of drunks earlier, but they had left. When it came time to close, he offered to stay while I closed and then walk me to my car, in case any of the rejected parties were waiting for me outside.

"He had been polite, never out of line, so I accepted his offer and let him stay to talk after closing while I cleaned up.

"I washed the dishes, wiped up the bar, and took the receipts to the safe. Generally, just the usual closing for the night. I figured we would just go out the back door together, since the front door was locked. He was parked in front, but I told him I would give him a ride around to the front to his car. He was very nice about it and thanked

me.

"After I was all finished, he said he would buy me a nightcap if I wanted one. I figured one drink would not hurt, so I accepted. Since the register was closed for the night, the sale would show up on the next day's receipts.

"That's when something went terribly wrong. I started to feel sick. In fact, I became dizzy and couldn't think straight. The next few hours were a fog. I have just an occasional snatch of pictures in my head of what was going on.

"When I awakened, hours later, I was in a hotel room, naked in bed. Wilkerson was in the shower. I was so horrified, I got dressed and ran out of the room.

"I called the police and we

149

all went back to the room. When Wilkerson answered the door, he acted like we were lovers and couldn't understand why I was upset. No one believed me."

Signed: Jacqueline M. Harper

The notes from the investigating officer stated that she'd appeared traumatized. She quit her job and refused to go back.

However, the file also had Wilkerson's statement, which said she'd insisted on going with him after closing the bar. He took her back to his hotel room and they went to bed. She was all over him, telling him what all she wanted him to do to her. They had sex several times and she wanted him to promise to see her again. He agreed to call her when he was back in town.

When he came out of the shower the next morning, police were at the door. He couldn't understand what her problem was since it was her idea to be with him in the first placc.

Donna finished reading the statements to Lou, and he whistled. "You have got to be kidding! Listen to this!" He took out his Vic's statement and started reading.

"This is dated two years ago, by the way. The Vic's name is Sally. Here is her statement:

> *"I was working the late shift at the Camelot Bar. It was slow that evening and the only patron left was a man who introduced himself as Henry Wilkerson. He sat at the bar, and we chatted while I jump-started my night-time cleanup. At closing time, he asked if he could stay and talk while I was cleaning. That way I would not be alone and he would walk me out back to my car. You don't find that kind of chivalry very often, so I said, 'Sure,' locked up the front door, and put up the 'Closed' sign.*

"After I finished my work, he offered to buy me a drink to close out the evening. I don't drink much, but I thought a glass of wine would be okay. That is when my night became a nightmare. I started feeling dizzy and a little sick to my stomach. I could swear the room was spinning. Everything was a fog. I felt someone pick me up and carry me somewhere. I was in such a daze that I didn't even care. Then things just blacked out.

"When I came to about five hours later, I was on the daybed back in the employees' lounge. I was naked—well, almost. And I had been raped. No doubt about it, he raped me.

Signed: Sally Gail Washington

"How's that for comparing notes?" Lou asked his attentive partner.

"Why that piece of…..he raped them both. This is no coincidence!" Donna was beyond amazed at what this man was capable of.

"Wilkerson's statement is a little different this time. He says she asked him to stay after closing, but he didn't feel too comfortable doing that, so he left. Since she had locked up the front door already, he left by the back, but another man was walking up the alley as he was leaving to go around front to his car. The reason he got away with it is that Denver had no reason to know about Kansas City—since no charges had been filed." Lou dropped the paperwork onto his desk and looked up at Donna.

Lou asked, "Why was your gal suspected of lying?"

"Says here, she was a partier and liked to have a good time. She admitted to going home with some men she would meet at parties, from time to time. What about yours, Lou?"

"Well, this was her second time claiming rape. The first was her ex-husband, who was

153

abusive. She had a restraining order against him, but she said he showed up one night to rape and beat her. His alibi was his brother—who swore the he was with him all night long. Yeah, right…." Even Lou was believing Wilkerson deserved to die.

"Well, we know we have a lowlife who is dead, but murder is just as illegal as drug trafficking and rape. You find your Vic, and I'll find mine. What a mess."

~~~

For the next two days, each detective searched the net trying to locate their apparent rape victims. They also ran searches for driver's licenses and social security numbers to help a long, drawn-out process since so many shared the same names. Lou was the first to succeed on Friday.

"I found Sally! She is working at another club now but is willing to speak with me. I have to say she is still angry that Wilkerson was not charged with her rape. She made an appointment to call me tomorrow afternoon after she wakes up. I'll let you know what I find out."

The Kansas City victim, Jacqueline, had left shortly after her ordeal. It was unknown why she left or where she went. Donna traced her girl backwards from Kansas City. Prior to going to Kansas City, Missouri, she had lived in Chicago. And it seemed she'd left Phoenix to go to Chicago. But, she'd gone to Phoenix from Houston. *Whew, this girl gets around!*

There were no incidences Donna could find in Chicago that involved Jacqueline, but in Phoenix, she'd been at a party that was busted for drugs. She was not charged with anything because she'd stated that she didn't know about the drugs and her drug test had come back negative. *Well, OK. She wasn't using drugs—at least not then.*

It was in Houston, Donna discovered, that Jacqueline was born and raised. Her parents,

155

Carl and Cassandra Harper, had been killed about two years previous in a head-on collision.

This was déjà vu somehow. She felt like she knew these people. For some reason, Donna knew their names. In fact, she was sure of it, but she couldn't figure out where or how.

Jacqueline had one sister and two brothers, also born in Houston. She would start there to see if anyone could help her find her rape victim.

She contacted the Houston P.D. to get the information on the death of the parents, and anything they could come up with on the family or friends. Donna was told it would be a few days before she would receive the info, but they would get it to her.

Donna called it a day and left work. The whole case was whirling around in her mind. When she reached home Friday night, she made a sandwich and lay down on her couch to think. It was all one big mess.

A scuzzball gets killed—and he was

murdered. I know it! No man with an arrogant ego like his would have done himself in! So, a scuzzball gets killed, and there are tons of people who would have wanted him to die.

Could an owner of any of the businesses he cashed out on have come back for revenge? After all, Wilkerson set them up to take the fall after he pulled a lot of money out of their businesses. That's a heck of a motive. I know I would want revenge.

Then there are the two raped girls. The man got away with two rapes we know of. Those women were chastised for their backgrounds, not for what happened to them. Then there is the rich, handsome Wilkerson saying, 'Gee, it ain't me, fellas! Can I buy you a drink?'

And now we come back to the wife, who also had reason to want him dead. With him gone, she no longer faced the humiliation of his constant cheating, and she would inherit a ton of money—let alone whatever life insurance he had.

157

Yep. It's time to talk to the wife again.

The same facts kept playing over and over in Donna's mind. Reviewing each one, she wasn't even aware of when she'd fallen asleep.

Donna awoke on her couch at ten in the evening. She took a shower and went to bed. This case was getting to her.

~~~

Saturday morning, Donna was ready to go at it again. Lou came into the office right behind her, but it was obvious he hadn't gotten as much sleep as she had.

"Everything okay?" She always worried about her friend and partner.

"Yes….no. Clarissa called last night and cried and cried. She thinks I don't love her, she thinks you and I are having an affair, and she thinks I'm accusing her of being a cheater because I want to find out if the baby is mine."

"Well, what did you tell her in response to all of those accusations?"

"Yes. No. No. That was about all she would let me say. When I said I had to work this Saturday, she hung up on me." Lou slumped down into his seat. He faced over his desk to Donna.

"I have a confession to make. This past week, since she has been gone, has been kind of nice. I mean, there is no arguing. Dinners are quiet, without accusations. No pressuring to get married. No pushing me to accept something I am not sure about.

"I am doubting how I initially thought I felt about her. I mean, being glad someone is gone can't be love, can it?" Lou felt guilty because he didn't feel bad.

"Well, I have to say, that's great! I mean, if you're not sorry she's gone, then don't let her move back in! It's obvious she is not the one for you, or you would pine away for her. Move past that part of your life. The baby is another story. If he or she is yours, then you can enjoy fatherhood without being unhappily married to the momma." Donna felt relief, and the smile on her face showed it.

Wow. Was he actually seeing what a pushy broad Clarissa is? Of course, he has the baby to consider, but I know he'll do the right thing when the time comes.

Lou chuckled. "Yeah, I guess so. I even moved some furniture back to where I had it before she moved in. I like it better that way. It's like this big weight off my shoulders. But I have to tell you: I do feel guilty because I don't feel bad!"

Both laughed and then turned back to the files on their desk. Donna made an appointment with Caroline Wilkerson for one o'clock that afternoon. Lou said he wanted to go, too. Then she left a message on Tracy's voicemail for a call back. It was time to find out why she'd lied.

There was some relief for both of them

when a bunch of paperwork got finished and put away. It was only eleven, so they decided to catch lunch before their appointment.

Lou was animated and joking—like old times. He seemed years younger and a whole lot happier than he had in a long while.

When his cell phone rang, his mood changed. Donna didn't know who it was, but judging from Lou's side of the conversation, it appeared that he was promising to meet someone at six that evening. After the call, Lou pretended it had never happened but remained more serious.

Lou finally got down to business. "So you think the wife did the guy in?"

"I don't know, but I do know that she had motive, motive, and then a whole lot more motive. I know I would probably have put a bullet in his skull!" Donna even laughed when she said it.

"Remind me never to marry a woman

who packs heat! Gads, girl. Your man would have to sleep with one eye open!" Lou kicked her under the table.

"Of course he would sleep with one eye open. That would be the only good eye he would have left if I caught him ogling some other woman!" She kicked him back. She really liked the man she had to spend most of her time with.

CHAPTER

13

Lou and Donna arrived at the Wilkerson home around one o'clock, Saturday afternoon. Once again she heard the beautiful chimes echoing throughout the house when she pushed the doorbell. Caroline answered immediately.

What a difference from the last time they'd been here. The widow looked stunning. Her makeup was perfect, and her beautiful clothes enhanced an already excellent figure. The happiness on her face was unmistakable.

Please, God. I'm begging you. Don't let it be this sweet woman. She suffered enough at his hands. Let her be happy for the rest of her life. Donna sent the prayer off just as she stepped inside the home.

"Welcome! Please, come in!" Caroline was cheerful and not the least bit sorry to see them. "How nice to see you again. Is that an acceptable way to act? That you are happy to see the Police?" She giggled.

"What I mean is, I am glad to see you under differ…. oh, forget it. Come in and sit down!" After Lou and Donna sat down on the same couch as before, Caroline went to the hall and raised her voice a bit. "Heddy, we have guests."

Caroline sat on the sofa across from them, the same sofa she'd sat on when told of her husband's death.

"Yes, Caroline. Can I get you

something?" Heddy, the housekeeper appeared at the door and then looked around at the detectives and smiled.

"Heddy, these are Detectives Lou McGregor and Donna Decker. I think you met them at the precinct. Could you please bring us something to drink?" Caroline said.

Hellos were exchanged, and Heddy went off to the kitchen. They could hear some commotion out in the back yard, and Donna mentioned it.

"Do you have a party going outside? Sounds like we're interrupting some fun."

"Oh, no, that's my daughter, Shana, and her swimming coach. Today is her lesson. She is three years old, and I want to make sure she can take care of herself if she should ever fall into a pool or lake. So far, she loves it." Caroline's eyes twinkled.

Heddy returned with sweet tea for them all and then disappeared. Lou was the one who started talking first.

"Mrs. Wilkerson…"

"Caroline. Nothing more, please."

"Caroline. And we are 'Lou' and 'Donna.' Okay? Thank you, and thank you for the tea. We have more questions, and, quite frankly, I have to warn you they may not be pretty. We're not here to make you unhappy again, but we have to know a few things."

Caroline became a bit pensive. "I understand, Lou. All this ugliness is not your fault. Please ask me what you will."

Donna blurted it out. "Were you aware your husband was cheating on you?"

The silence ticked on for more than a minute. Caroline was not shocked, but her eyebrows went up, and she kept glancing at the floor as if she were looking to find something. Whatever it was, she didn't find it.

"No. I was not aware of it, but I am not surprised. Detectives, you have to understand a few things about my marriage. It was a marriage in appearance only. Heddy said she had explained that to you. We did not even share the same bedroom and had not for more than three years. Did I know he cheated? No. Do I care? No." Caroline was composed again—saddened, but not unhappy.

"So your marriage was in name only? Was it always that way or did something happen to make it work out that way?" Donna didn't know if she had asked the right question to get the answer she needed.

"Cathleen. Cathleen happened." Now sadness overtook her face. She didn't wait for the obvious question about who that might be.

"Cathleen was our precious, beautiful little girl. When Henry found out I was pregnant, he begged me to get an abortion. He did not want the 'father' image attached to him. I refused to give up my baby. We never... We never made love again after that. The little girl was five months old when she died—crib death.

167

"Henry thought that was the perfect occasion to reactivate our failed marriage, but I would have none of it. The man I loved no longer existed if he ever had at all. And I was not going to pretend he cared about me." Caroline was now sitting completely back into the sofa, taking a deep breath now and then.

Donna wasn't sure what to think. "And Shana?"

"Adopted."

"Okay. Caroline, did you have life insurance on your husband?"

Caroline was obviously surprised by the question and sat mute for a couple of moments.

She then giggled and said, "Yes, one-million dollars, to be exact. But I didn't take it out on him. He did it on both of us. I had the same insurance package. It had occurred to me he did it to collect on mine one day, but was blessed that never happened."

Lou and Donna exchanged glances.

Caroline continued, "To answer your unspoken question, yes, I am set financially. The mortgage had life insurance on it so if he died, the house got paid off—completely. We had a lot of money in the bank to start with, and, really, the life insurance money was not the largest amount by any means.

"And yes, I have collected the life insurance money—two days ago. I also put a check in the mail yesterday. Half of the insurance was given to my church. I doubt Pastor Tim has even received it yet. They can do better things with it than I can. The other half was put in a trust for my daughter." She was composed again, and some of the happiness had returned to her eyes.

Donna and Lou both felt they were going in the wrong direction.

"I have a couple more questions for your sister. I've left a message for her, but she hasn't called me back. Do you know where she is?" Donna was watching for any sign of fear. None

169

came.

"I have no idea where she is. She always has that phone with her. But then the battery could have gone dead or something. They do that at the most inconvenient times, don't they?" Caroline smiled as if recalling a memory.

"This is very good tea!" Donna said to change the subject.

"Thank you! I actually brew it myself! Can you believe that? Someone actually brews tea from scratch anymore?" The little-girl giggle that came out of Caroline had all of them laughing!

"Well, this is certainly worth the time and effort!" Lou was starting to like the lady a lot.

"Mommy!" A stunning little girl came running into the room with a bathing suit on and a towel around her. Her cobalt-blue eyes were in contrast to her long, dark, and dripping-wet hair.

"I jumped off the side right into Becky's arms! Really, Mommy! I *jumped* just cause I wanted to!"

"Wow! You did! Wow! You know *what?* You will get a big treat with dinner tonight, just for doing that! I am so proud of you!

"Darling, I want you to meet a couple of friends of mine. This is Lou McGregor and Donna Decker. Lou and Donna, this is my daughter, Shana." Caroline's pride for her daughter was more than obvious.

The little girl walked over to Lou and put out her right hand for him to shake.

"How do you do, Mr. Lou McGregor?" Shana was so serious that Lou broke out laughing and shook the little girl's hand.

"I am doing well, thank you. And how about yourself?" He melted at her very presence.

"I am also doing well." Then she walked over to Donna with her right hand out.

"How do you do…?" She glanced back at her mother with questions in her eyes.

"Donna Decker." Caroline said and

171

smiled.

"How do you do, Donna Decker? You sure are *pretty!*"

Donna choked and then said with a big smile, "I am doing very well, Shana, and thank you for the wonderful compliment! Coming from you, that means a lot." Carrying on the formal atmosphere, she added, "And I hope you are doing well!"

Shana smiled and said, "Yes, I am fine." She then turned and ran into her mother's arms.

Lou spoke next, "Has she always been so perfectly mannered? I thought kids were more… well… self-centered, I guess."

Caroline let out a laugh and said, "Yes! I am afraid my little one here has given a really bad name to 'terrible twos' because she has always been so sweet."

Donna got up. "Thank you for your time, Caroline. Have a great day. Oh, don't get up. Hold onto your baby, and we'll find the door!" She waved goodbye to Shana, and they shut the front door behind them.

"Well," Lou said as they got into his car to return to work. "I think we can close *that* door."

"Yeah. What a lousy marriage she had. Wow. I can't think of a name bad enough for a man who would want his wife to abort his own child because of appearances! How disgusting is that?" Donna couldn't get her brain around this guy. Not even a little.

But then they turned around and adopted? That doesn't make sense, either…

"Looks like Mrs. …*Caroline*… came out of it okay, though. I am glad about that. Can you believe that child?" Lou laughed out loud. Then he became quiet. It had dawned on him that maybc hc was trying to throw *his* own child away, too.

"Lou, don't even *GO* there! I *know* what you are thinking and there is absolutely *no* comparison. You and I both know if it is your child, you will be a wonderful father! Now knock it off before I have to pistol-whip you!" Donna slammed him in his shoulder as he was driving.

"OW! Seriously woman, you are going to be the death of me, yet!"

"You keep pushing your luck, and I'll make sure of it!" Donna was relieved to see the sadness gone and the smile return to his face.

CHAPTER

14

Just as they walked back into the precinct, their captain hollered for them to come to his office.

When they stepped inside, Captain George Parry said, "Shut the door."

Lou and Donna gave each other the '*Now* what?' look. After they sat down, he asked about their investigation and how things were coming together. After they brought him up to date, he dropped his bombshell.

"You know Stella Douglas? She is one of the people you interviewed for your case, right?

It was Lou who spoke up. "Yes, we interviewed her. But, really Captain, she isn't…"

"Take a chill, Lou, I'm not finished. Seems a complaint came in today *from* her. She says someone is stalking her, and she is afraid for her life after what happened at the church."

"Stalking her?" It was Donna whose mouth was open now.

The captain slapped a folder in front of them.

"I know you two have your hands full right now, but I am assigning it to you since you already know the Vic, and it may be a part of your current investigation."

Donna picked up the folder, thanked the Captain, and went back to their facing desks.

She read it out loud to Lou.

"It says here, she has been followed going to school and going to work for the past week. She can't make out who the man is, but he seems 'big.'" Donna looked up with a small smile at that word. "Stella said he drives a pickup but can't identify anything about it. Says he stays way back from her, but he is always there."

"Looks like we need to talk to our young lady again." Lou didn't like this whole thing. What could be going on? This girl didn't have anything that anyone would want to steal, and she sure wasn't ransom material. The only thing left was….

Lou didn't want to go there. *Sex rings are a plague upon society and the world, but Stella seems to be a little old for that sort of thing. Generally the ages are between eight and thirteen. Stella is what, nineteen? But, then again, she looks much younger. Who would be responsible for such a thing?*

Donna called Stella and made an

MURDER FOR A MOMENT

appointment for later in the afternoon. Saturday had turned busy for the partners. Stella said she didn't have any more classes, plus she wasn't expected at work today. Gabe took her out to lunch, but she is home to stay now.

The next couple of hours were spent checking and rechecking the facts they had. Lou was still waiting a call from Sally, scheduled for the next day, when she promised to answer any questions he had.

Sally called Lou and told him she'd been called in to work, but she would have Monday off and would call him then. Lou didn't like it, but there was no choice but to put off the interview.

Donna had not received any information from Houston about Jacqueline. That was not surprising. She was sure her case had not been put on the top of the pile—but she planned to keep harassing them until she got what she needed.

By three-thirty, they were both tired of sitting and staring at the paperwork. It was time for their appointment with Stella. Getting out of her chair and stretching was the most pleasurable thing Donna had done all day.

At four o'clock, they pulled up to the small, but neat, brick house on the south side of Wichita. It had a one-car attached garage, which must have been holding Stella's car because it was not outside. They parked in the driveway.

As they were walking up to the front door, it flew open, and Stella ran out and grabbed Donna, giving her a big hug and starting to cry. She looked like a frightened child.

"Thank you so much for coming. I didn't know who else to call I have been so scared!"

Donna held her for a moment and said, "No one is going to hurt you on our watch, Stella. We won't let that happen." Donna looked over at Lou, who nodded his agreement. "Let's go inside and you can tell us everything that is going on."

When Stella was in control again, she

179

walked them into the house and they sat down in the small living room.

"I just keep seeing this truck following me. It looks like a pickup, but I can't tell anything about it. I know I'm not crazy. I saw him four days in a row following me to school, and then yesterday when I went to work and last night's class.

"I turn, he turns. I am so scared. Do you think it has anything to do with that man who was found at the church?" Stella's nerves had her talking fast, but she finally got it all out and stopped.

"We have no reason to believe the two are connected. Stella, it could—and I am just saying it *could*—be a coincidence. Do you know of anyone that you might have offended or hurt in any way? Can you think of anyone who would want to scare you?" Donna was trying to cover all the bases.

"Oh, please God, I hope I have not offended anyone. Not that I know of. Why would anyone do that to another human being? I am really scared."

Lou spoke up. "Okay, so we don't know anything about this person. What we need to do is catch him in the act. Would you have a problem with that, Stella?"

"Uh… What do you mean, 'catch him in the act'? The act of what?" Stella's eyes were saucers.

"Well, if you are going to work or school, you can call us when you see he is following you so we can apprehend him. Catching him following you is the only way to find out who it is." Donna hoped she wasn't scaring her any more than she already was.

What happened next surprised both Lou and Donna.

"Of course. What am I *thinking?*" The mature woman in Stella suddenly appeared. "Of course, I will just call you when I see him following me again. I have no reason to be afraid of this person. So far he hasn't even tried to get close to me.

"I apologize for being such a baby. Stuff happens in life, and we just have to face them." Stella was sitting upright and was not at all the scared little girl they'd seen just a few minutes before.

"That would be great, Stella. Call Donna's cell phone or mine if you see this truck again, or you can call the main number on the front." Lou handed her a card with their cell phone numbers written on the back.

"Of course. Thank you so much for caring. I do feel much better. I know you will catch this guy. I just know it." Stella was back to her smiling self.

Lou and Donna got up to leave. Donna added one more bit of advice: "Don't go out at night unless it is an emergency, Stella. Just a precaution until this is over. Okay? Not even on a date with Gabe."

Donna watched to make sure Stella was paying attention, "Have him come over here, but you are not to leave the house after dark, not for work, not for class. Tell them you are not available for a while. Your professors can send your assignments by email—you know that. Just be home by dark."

Lou and Stella both laughed as Donna sounded like a mother giving orders to a teenager.

Stella agreed and hugged Donna. She waved at them as they walked out to the car.

As Lou drove off, he looked at Donna and asked, "What do you think?"

"Well, I couldn't say anything in front of her, but remember that comment Wilkerson made to her? The one about 'any man would pay for her' kind of comment? It may be a long shot, but what if Wilkerson was involved in prostitution—and we have no reason to believe he was *not* involved because of his business history!

"Maybe he *did* sell her to someone and

183

was going to deliver the goods but died before he could make good on the deal. Now that buyer wants what he paid for." Donna was feeling sick to her stomach.

"Oh, crap, girl. You don't think….? It had crossed my mind earlier, but she is quite a bit older than girls that are bought and sold, don't you think?"

"I don't know. She's nineteen, but you have to admit she doesn't look more than fourteen or so! It also could be the 'virgin' thing that he sold. It isn't really a stretch to suspect her of being an innocent virgin, now, is it? But we will have to keep an eye on her, a close eye. I am going to ask Parry for a stakeout, at least for a few days." Donna was already on her phone, calling the captain.

She explained the problem to her captain as well as her request for a stakeout. After her conversation with Parry, she snapped her phone shut and turned to Lou.

"He agreed. He is sending someone over to keep an eye on her house. They should be in place in about an hour. It makes me feel better having a watch on her, I have to tell you."

They were silent all the way back to the station. Both were engrossed in their own thought concerning this disturbing development. Was someone trying to kidnap this young lady? If so, why? But right now, the more important question was *who*?

Since it was after five, Lou dropped Donna off at her car and drove away.

As she left in her car, she remembered Lou had made an appointment with someone for six. Maybe he was meeting with his girlfriend. Donna wanted Lou to do whatever made him happy. She really wanted that for him.

She just wasn't sure he would be able to find it with Clarissa.

MURDER FOR A MOMENT

CHAPTER

15

Monday morning Lou came to work with an attitude that Donna couldn't understand. He almost seemed angry. She couldn't imagine what may have caused it.

She had not heard from him yesterday since they'd had Sunday off. She did some laundry and then went grocery shopping since she had little left in the house to eat. It was a quiet, yet productive, day.

Now, they buried themselves in the newest paperwork, and she let him be.

Close to noon, Sally called from Colorado. He spoke with her for about half an hour before hanging up. Afterwards, he seemed more like himself as he concentrated on the case.

"I believe this girl, Donna. Wilkerson raped her, alright. The same story as in Kansas City. They have a drink together, girl passes out while he is the only one present, next morning he is gone, and she has been raped. Wilkerson said it was consensual sex and that he didn't know what she did after he left. They believed him. Man—what is it with some people? Just because a girl works at a bar doesn't make it okay to rape her!"

"Yeah, I hear ya." Donna was fuming too. "I am going to get on the horn and kick some Houston butt about my Vic."

Speaking with the Houston Police Department, she was told her request had been assigned to Detective Larry Vestom. He was not in, but she left a message on his voice mail to call her back today.

After a couple of minutes reading from a file, Donna looked up to see that Lou was apparently far away in his thoughts and that his face was sad. At least he was no longer angry.

"What do you hear from Clarissa these days?" Donna was looking down at her file, trying to act casual.

"What? Clarissa? Remember I told you she called me Saturday morning and ended up hanging up on me when I told her I had to work? Yeah, well, she came into my house while I was working and took some money I had there. She left a note saying her mother needed the help since she had moved back in with her."

"Lou! You have to change the locks on your door. You can't just let someone who is not living in your house have complete access to everything!" Donna was horrified at the thought.

"I know. I doubt seriously her poor mother got a dime of the money, either. I will take care of that. I have thought of a lot of things lately that I would never have a couple of weeks ago. Like I told you, I have enjoyed her being gone. My nights are actually quiet and peaceful. My mother won't say so, but she is happier when I go over to her house alone." Lou shook his head. Anger appeared in his eyes again. He had to get his life back in order—and soon.

Suddenly, he stood up and leaned over his desk, close to his partner. "Donna, cover for me for a couple of hours. There are some things I have decided need to get done, and done now."

"Sure. I understand," she said as she watched him walk out the door. She had plenty to keep her busy in the meantime. With this case, she had enough to keep her busy for a long time.

The phone on her desk rang.

"Detective Decker. Yes, Detective Vestom! Thank you for getting back with me. What have you got on Jackie Harper?" Donna was excited to be getting some information.

"Sorry I took so long to get back with you, Detective, but we have been hit with three murders this week, and I am stretched pretty thin. And it's Larry." His voice even sounded tired.

"I do appreciate whatever time you can give me. We have a murder here, too, and I have to tell you, Larry, we are not spinning our wheels. That would be good news. We seem to be going *backwards*. This case is driving us crazy.

Vestom laughed out loud. "I understand completely, Detective. That pretty much explains how we feel around here, this week.

"Well, I don't have much, but it may get you closer to finding her. She was here but moved away about fifteen months ago from what I can ascertain. Don't know where she went, but I did find a relative you might get more info from. His name is Mason Henry Harper. He is her brother. He owns Harper Construction Corp. here in Houston and is very successful. I haven't been able to reach him, but here is his phone number."

"Thank you. I appreciate your help, Larry. I'll take it from here." Donna said her goodbyes and dialed the Houston phone number he'd given her.

When the receptionist answered, she identified herself and asked for Mason Harper. Surprisingly, she was put right through.

"Mason here." The voice was no-nonsense and all-business.

Donna identified herself and told him she was trying to find his sister, Jackie Harper.

There was silence on the line for a long while. Just when Donna figured she had lost the connection, she heard his voice.

"I don't know why everyone is looking for her, and I don't care. I will tell you what I told the gentleman a couple of weeks ago. I have nothing to say. Period. If you want any information, you will have to contact my sister. Her number is 316…"

"What? The area code is 316? That is the area code here in Wichita." Donna needed to make sure she heard him right.

"Yeah. The number is for my sister, Cassie Harper, in Wichita."

Donna took down the number and hung up.

Now she knew why the name of Cassie's parents sounded so familiar! The mother was Cassandra Harper. In Wichita, there was a TV news personality named Cassandra Harper. She went by Cassie most of the time. That's where Donna had heard the name. And it turns out, she is the sister to the woman they were looking for.

Hopefully I will be able to get more information from her than from her brother. I don't know why, but he was pretty touchy about the whole thing. And someone has already contacted him about her....? Who else would be looking for her...?

Donna dialed the number, and a woman

answered immediately.

"Cassie Harper."

"Cassie, this is Detective Decker with the Wichita Police Department. I am trying to find your sister, Jackie Harper. I was wondering if you could help me locate her."

Again Donna got silence on the phone. *What is up with this?*

"Detective, I can't talk here. Can you meet me at Starbucks at Twin Lakes Shopping Center in about 20 minutes?"

Donna said she could and left the precinct. Driving to Twin Lakes, she couldn't help but wonder what the big deal was about where Jackie was. *What is the big mystery here?*

Spotting Cassie sitting next to the window was easy since she had seen her pretty face on the news almost every day for several years. Donna walked up to the table.

"I'm Detective Decker. May I sit down?"

Cassie looked up and motioned with her hand for Donna to sit. Cassie had a latte in front of her that seemed like it hadn't been touched.

"You look a lot like my sister. Dark hair and bright blue eyes. Did you want a latte or something, Detective Decker, is it?" Cassie's voice was quiet and sad.

"Yes, Donna Decker. And no. I'm fine."

Cassie started with, "Why are you looking for my sister?"

"Cassie, I will be the first to tell you everything, but I can't do it today. I'm very sorry, but it is important I find..."

"Jackie would have been 24 years old this month..."

"*Would* have been?" Donna was startled by Cassie's statement.

"Yes. Jackie committed suicide a little over a year ago."

MURDER FOR A MOMENT

CHAPTER

16

Cassie Harper continued, "Detective, to talk about her, I am going to have to give you some background. I hope you are not in a hurry because I don't know any other way to do this. The last time I spoke about her, I just spit it out, and it left me empty. I can't do that this time." Cassie was uncomfortable, but friendly.

Still stunned by the pronouncement, Donna nodded her consent to the story, so Cassie

197

continued.

"Jackie was born six years after me. She was the 'surprise' baby in our family. I have two older brothers, thirty-five and thirty-two. I just turned 30. Jackie was always the restless one. She started college but just couldn't get her head around it. She quit and told all of us she just wanted to see America and live her life. That's how she put it." Cassie turned and was staring out the window again.

"For a couple of years, she did just that. She didn't tell us much about her travels, but she came home for Christmas, Mother's Day, and Father's Day. I talked to her about once a month on her cell, so it all seemed to work out.

"Then she decided to go home and spend some time with our parents. I was thrilled to hear it. She moved back into her old room. Mom told me she was withdrawn and sad. Jackie denied it all, of course, but whatever drew her home was, apparently, not a happy memory." Cassie was fighting tears now. Donna didn't know what was coming, but it obviously was painful to Cassie.

"Mom and Dad were going somewhere, and some drunk crossed over and hit them head on. Both died instantly." Cassie choked on her tears. Donna could see she was having a hard time talking about that unbearable event in her life. Losing her parents was something Donna could not even get her brain around. She almost could feel the pain Cassie had. Almost.

Breathing deeply and dabbing the tears from her eyes, Cassie continued. "We all were devastated, of course. They were only in their upper fifties... so much ahead of them. But I think Jackie took it the hardest. Being the baby, maybe. I don't know....

"Anyway, she was in no condition to stay in Houston, in that house, all by herself. I talked her into coming to Wichita with me. Mom's house sold in two days. Can you believe it? The Realtor said nice homes in Houston were in heavy demand.

"The entire estate was settled in one month. Mom and Dad had everything in their wills set up in a trust, so it was easy on us kids.

"I wanted Jackie to live with me in my condo, but she insisted on having her own place. She certainly had the funds to live on her own from Mom and Dad passing. She was trying to figure out what she wanted to do with her life and even talked about going back to college.

"She rented an apartment not far from here, in fact." Again Cassie's voice trailed off while she looked up at the sky through the window. It was almost if she thought she would see something there.

Cassie didn't say anything else. She just stared out the window, lost in her own misery.

"What happened, Cassie?" Donna spoke softly to bring her back to reality.

"Oh, I don't know. She seemed fine. We saw each other every couple of days, and I thought she was happy. You know, picking her life back up. She even wanted to start going back to church again. We used to go with our parents all the time, but after we left home, it was left up to us if we still wanted to.

"She said she was listening to some preacher on the radio and wanted to find a church locally that preached the same message. She was really excited when she found just the right church she wanted to go to. Jackie said it preached the 'complete' message of the cross, whatever that means. It was the only one in Wichita, she said."

Donna's eyes became saucers as her eyebrows met her hairline! *Whaaaat? No way. There is no way she could have been going to "that" church! No way!*

Cassie said, "It was located somewhere off of…."

"South Seneca." Donna's voice was louder than she meant for it to be.

"Yes. *How* did you know that?" This shook Cassie out of her reverie, and she was staring at Donna's shocked look.

It took a few seconds, but Donna got it back under control and said, "Go on, Cassie. If she was so happy, why…."

"Well, the happiness lasted about two weeks. Then when I would call and ask her to meet me for dinner or a movie, she would decline. She wasn't well, or she had a headache, or something. She just changed. I still don't get it. She was so depressed. How can going to church make you so unhappy?

"Anyway, after a couple of days of her not answering her phone, I went to her apartment. Her car was there, but there was no answer. I was so worried by then that I got the manager to open her door. And… that's… that's…."

"It's okay, Cassie. How did she die?"

"Pills. She had a prescription for sleeping pills, and the bottle was empty. She had taken those things for years." The tears were coming again. Then suddenly Cassie's face became angry.

"Why would she do such a thing? Why would she hurt everyone so much? How could she be so selfish?" Cassie put her head down and let the tears come. People at nearby tables turned to look at them.

Donna held Cassie's hand across the table and waited until she was in control again.

"Anyway, I had a moving company pack everything and clear out the apartment. I had it all moved into my basement and haven't looked at it since. I just can't bear to.

"You haven't told me why you wanted to find her. She wasn't the kind of girl that had police looking for her!" Cassie was defending her lost sister, even now.

"No, Cassie, she didn't do anything wrong. I had wanted to get some information from her about something that happened a long time ago. I can't go into it all now, I'm afraid." Donna couldn't feel sorrier for this young lady who had to smile for the camera every day.

She thanked Cassie for taking the time to tell her the truth. As she was leaving, Donna promised she would tell her why she was asking, as soon as she could. Cassie accepted that with a nod.

Stunned by the fact that Jackie went to the same church, Donna's mind was racing, trying to put the pieces together while she drove back to her office. Obviously, Jackie was no longer a suspect in Wilkerson's death, but this turn of events was mind boggling. Before she even realized it, she was back at the precinct.

That's when two things happened at once. First, Lou walked in right behind her, and second, the captain came out of his office and yelled, "Where have you two been? Get in here!"

"Sorry, I… we... didn't have time to tell you, captain, but we had to meet with an informant to get information for our case." Donna could see Lou looking at her from her peripheral vision.

"Yeah," Lou jumped in with a stupid grin.

"Don't want to turn down free info!"

Donna and Captain Parry both looked at him like he was crazy.

"Who did you find?" Captain was looking straight at Lou.

"Our victim in Kansas City has a sister here in town, and we met with her." Donna answered for her partner.

"Yeah," Lou said. The captain was still looking at him.

Captain Parry sighed, shook his head, and said, "Get out of here, both of you, and get some work done."

They were very happy to oblige.

When they reached their facing desks, Lou leaned over and said, "Thanks for covering my butt. I owe you."

"You owe me for a lot more than that, Batman." Donna smiled sweetly at her partner, who now looked a little worried.

"So, what is this about a sister? You *are* talking about Jackie Harper? You found her sister?" Lou wanted in on everything now.

"As I said. Yes. Yes." Donna pretended to be looking through a file.

"Okay, fun's over. Give it up." Both Lou and Donna laughed at this.

Donna spent the next half hour telling Lou everything she'd found out about Jackie, the church she'd gone to, and her suicide. Also the fact that she was no longer on the suspect list.

"You are telling me that she went to the same church? Girl, you *cannot* be serious!"

"Yes. Yes." Donna couldn't resist one more tease.

She added, "Could that have been what caused her to commit suicide? She ran into her rapist—at church, of all places?"

"Sounds like it to me. What are the

chances….?" Lou's heart went out to her.

"After all she had been through. Being raped, having the police blame the victim, going home only to lose both her parents at the same time. Moving here to start a new life then run into the man who raped you. Crap, Donna. I might have done the same thing."

"Or killed *him.* That's probably where *my* mind would have been. But we know Jackie didn't do it." This is one of those rare cases where Donna didn't really care who killed the man. He deserved it.

But, then again, murder was murder…. Her thoughts were interrupted by Lou.

"You know, as interesting as this information is, it still doesn't get us any closer to who killed Wilkerson. We are right back where we were more than ten days ago."

Frustration showed on them both, but Donna wasn't letting go just yet.

"I want to go out to the apartment complex where she lived and speak with the manager. Cassie said that was who let her into the apartment."

She pulled up the police report of Jackie's death from the year before to obtain her address.

"Okay, let's do it." Lou grabbed his jacket and headed for the door.

This time they stopped by the chief's office and announced their departure.

CHAPTER

17

Finding the Twin Lakes Apartment manager's office was easy. Signs were everywhere pointing to the right place. Actually, the office was very close to where Jackie's apartment had been. When they entered, a young lady smiled at them.

"Good afternoon! You must be looking for an apartment? I'll bet you guys are newlyweds!" Miss Chirpy was instantly annoying.

Before Donna could take a slice out of her tongue, Lou knew he had to save her. "We need to see the manager, please?"

"Oh, is anything wrong? Something I can help you with? I am hap…"

"Just the *manager.*" Donna had a no-nonsense look on her face as she shoved her badge into Miss Chirpy's face.

"Oh, just a moment, please." The girl barely whispered and disappeared into another room.

A moment later, a tall, stocky woman emerged. The room instantly became smaller.

"I'm Priscilla Walters. I understand you are police of some kind?" Her voice was naturally loud and authoritative.

"Mrs. Walters, I am Detective McGregor, and this is Detective Decker. We are here about Jackie Harper. She used to…." Lou didn't get the chance to finish.

"That poor girl. Yes, that was such a tragedy. Such a beautiful girl. I want you to know that rarely happens here at Twin La…."

"She lived very close to the office here. Did you ever notice if she had many visitors?" Donna was in no mood for idle gossip.

"Well, no. Not that I am aware of. Except that one really handsome guy who came to visit her a couple of times."

Lou jumped in. "What guy? What did he look like? Do you have a name? What kind of car did he drive?"

Mrs. Walters realized she'd hit on something important. "No. I don't know his name. He was average in height. Nice-looking man, that's for sure. Dressed very nicely, even in casual clothes he seemed well dressed. Drove an expensive car. One of those imports."

Lou offered, "Mercedes?"

"Yeah, that one. Like I said, he obviously had the bucks—know what I mean?" Priscilla gave Lou a smile full of crooked teeth.

"Did you see the two of them together often?"

"No. Actually, I can't say I ever saw them together at all. I mean, he must have been her boyfriend, or she wouldn't have given him a key to her unit."

Donna asked, "Key? How do you know he had a key to her place?"

Priscilla Walters smiled again and said, "Well, I was walking my dog when I ran into him coming out of her apartment. Since her car was not there, I assumed he had a key to come and go as he liked. When he saw me, he smiled, winked, and walked on to his car." Mrs. Walter's eyes suddenly got big. She turned to Donna and said, "Come to think of it, that was earlier in the day that she… before… you know…"

"Before she killed herself? He was here the day she killed herself?" Lou had to make sure they were on the same page. The woman nodded back at him, not smiling any more.

"Would you recognize him if you saw a picture?" Donna didn't know what to think, but it just might be someone they knew.

"Well… I guess so. Yeah, I think so."

Donna left Lou standing there as she ran back to their car. In the back seat, she rummaged through some of their files until she came to the one with the photos. Grabbing one, she ran back in.

"Is this the man?" A little out of breath, Donna was anxious for an answer.

"Well, my, yes. That's him! How in the world did you know? If he's still available, I have a niece who…." Blanche was definitely pleased to see his picture.

Lou interrupted and thanked her for her cooperation. He turned his partner around and back out the door. There was silence as they walked to the car. Once inside, they looked at each other and at the same time said, "Wilkerson!"

Once back at their desks, they were buzzing with ideas and "what ifs."

"What if Wilkerson approached her and somehow made amends?"

"What if Jackie invited him to her place to talk?"

"What if she invited him to her place in order to kill him for what he did?"

"What if…."

"Wait! What did you just say? That maybe she planned on killing him? Maybe it was the other way around! Hold it right there...." Donna was letting the thoughts swirl in her mind.

"What if Jackie didn't know he was even *in* her place? What if he used some of his burglary tools to enter when she was gone so he could kill *her?*

It was Lou who jumped in next. "Good Lord, girl. Are you saying she didn't kill herself but was murdered by Wilkerson?"

"Why not? She was raped by this man, and he got away with it. She lost her parents, moved to Wichita to be close to her sister, and start over with her life. She wants to start going to church, and what happens? She runs into her rapist! At church!

"Remember what Hawk said? That he wouldn't let his wife even talk to women? Didn't he say…?" Donna didn't get to finish.

"That some pretty brunette woman was trying to talk to Caroline, and he came charging up to remove her from the church. What do you want to bet it was Jackie? Maybe Jackie was trying to tell, or even warn, Caroline about the man she was married to, and Wilkerson had to stop her! Permanently!"

Both sat across from each other's desks and stared, as if they could read their partner's mind. Such thoughts were opening up an entirely different bag of worms, but they couldn't deny there was merit.

They spent the rest of the afternoon going over how it all could have gone down. They pulled the autopsy report and the crime scene report. They went over every detail until they discovered what they were looking for.

With Wilkerson's known background, they were pretty sure he'd gone into Jackie's apartment that day to put GHB into a bottle of wine that he knew she would open and drink that night.

Lou jumped in with, "While in her apartment, he must have found her bottle of sleeping pills on her bedside table. He could have forced her to take the pills. Or, making note of the drug involved, he would have had no trouble getting his hands on the same substance to use against her."

"Then, he would have watched the apartment window after she got home to give her time to drink the tainted wine and become unconscious. After the allotted time, he would then have gone back into her place, using the same tools he did before!" Donna's mind was a runaway train!

"Finding her passed out, he put her on the bed. He could have injected her with an overdose of the liquid form of her sleeping pills…"

"Or forced them down her throat."

"Probably enough to kill ten people, like the toxicology report states. If he brought his own drug, he would have emptied her prescription bottle into his pocket, took the contaminated wine and left Tracy to die." Lou realized he hadn't taken a breath.

The two detectives were smiling at each other now. Wilkerson took the contaminated wine—that was his mistake. The toxicology report showed wine in her system at time of death, but no wine bottle was found, full or empty, anywhere in the apartment. That little fact had not been noticed during the investigation more than a year ago.

The assumption that she'd downed all of those drugs with wine no longer worked. Someone else had to have been there, and they knew who it was.

After their discoveries, they both made copious notes in the order they would need them. Then they knocked on the chiefs door.

After they were all comfortable in their chairs, they spent the next two hours going over each detail, explaining how they'd come to each conclusion. When it was over, Chief Parry agreed with them.

He congratulated them on a job well done and reopened Jackie Harper's death investigation. The new information was added, making it an unsolved homicide. He also added Henry Wilkerson's name as the prime suspect.

Parry frowned and said, "I would give that previous detective a royal ass chewing, but the guy retired six months back. That wine bottle not being there was a huge oversight and should never have happened."

Donna remembered how pained, and angry, her sister had been over what she thought her sister had done. It was time to call Cassie and let her know Jackie wasn't a quitter. Quite the opposite, she was a fighter—and she almost won.

When it was all over, both Lou and Donna were exhausted but pleased. They now knew what really had happened to Jackie Harper.

Lou left the precinct and headed home. Donna was going to do the same thing after she made a phone call. Cassie and her family had a right to know.

She called her at home. When Cassie was told the truth, she screamed into the phone. Donna couldn't blame her but hoped she wasn't now deaf in that ear. Cassie must have thanked her eight times before she hung up. There was no doubt about it; it was Donna's pleasure.

Now she could go home and get a good night's sleep.

MURDER FOR A MOMENT

CHAPTER

18

The airplane was coming down straight at her. People were scrambling to get out of the way, but Donna's feet were frozen to the ground. Why was it coming at her? What had she done to deserve this? She used to like flying, but she knew in her heart, she would never fly again. The ring of the wings wouldn't stop... ring... ring... ring.... ri...

At three-thirty in the morning, Donna's

phone rang, jerking her out of some outrageous dream that didn't make sense. When she answered, it was the precinct. They caught the man stalking Stella! When they found him watching her place in the middle of the night, he was arrested.

Instantly awake, she told them to contact Lou and get him down there. Donna knew she would arrive before he did!

On the drive to the station, Donna's nerves were working overtime. Who could this creep be? Well, she was about to find out, and she couldn't wait to throw the book at him.

Lou and Donna walked in almost at the same moment. After grabbing the file for this case, they headed for interview room three, where they were told he was being held.

They charged into the room like they were the cavalry when they were stopped in their tracks at the room's occupant.

There sat Hawk Benton.

Donna was the first to find her voice.

"What are *you* doing here? What were you doing following *Stella?*" Anger spit out with every word.

"Well, lookie here! The man who accuses another man of being a pervert is one himself!" Lou's mind was reeling with this new information.

"I'm no pervert!" Hawk didn't have anything else to say.

"Really? A sweet nineteen-year-old girl is being stalked, and the stalker isn't a pervert?" Lou was rubbing every word in. "Tell, me, Hawk. What is the name you would give it? *Sicko? Disgusting?* What would it be?"

"Look! I was just keeping an eye on her so nothing would happen to her." Hawk's voice was low and unsure.

"Okaaaay then…," Lou started but didn't get to finish.

"Hawk, what the hell were you doing

223

stalking Stella?" Donna was furious, remembering the look on Stella's face when she'd run out of her house, right into Donna's arms.

"I just…."

"What, you jerk? You thought you might get some of that?" It was Lou who was in his face this time.

"No!"

"Really? You don't think she's young enough, or what?"

"Leave me alone. I didn't do anything wrong."

"Not a problem, Hawk. We turn pedophiles back out on the street all the time!"

"I am not a pedophile!"

"Oh? That's right. You aren't a pedophile because she's older than 18! Do you normally go for younger, Hawk?"

"Stop it. Just stop it. I was just trying to

keep her safe!"

"Really? And why would that *be*, Hawk…?"

"Because she's my daughter!"

The room went silent. Dead silent. Both Lou and Donna backed away from him like he was an alien and just stared. The moments passed. Many moments.

Lou and Donna then looked from each other to Hawk and back to each other. Had they heard that right? *Daughter?* Stella was his *daughter?*

After what seemed an hour and could only have been minutes, Donna quietly said, "What do you mean, she's your daughter?"

In a voice hardly above a whisper, Hawk said, "What do you think I mean? Stella is my daughter. I heard her talking about her grandmother passing away, and I knew the name. It was the mother of my girlfriend, all

225

those years ago. Her grandmother was a nice lady. Sorry she passed.

"Stella's mother, Trudy, invited me over to her place one night to tell me she was pregnant. She was about twenty-five at the time, as I recall. If there ever was a woman I wanted to marry, it was her. I loved her, I really did, but I knew I couldn't be a father.

"My father beat me so bad and was drunk all the time. I just figured that is what I would be like and didn't want no kid to go through what I did. I was in my early thirties at the time and still scared to give life a try. So I ran. I disappeared in the night, thinking I had saved the kid by doing so. I didn't come back all these twenty years." Hawk now had tears running down his cheeks, but didn't seem to care.

"Imagine my hearing the name 'Goldie Parker' from so long ago…

"After Stella was telling some other girls about her background—how she was raised by her Grandma Goldie after her mother died of cancer—I just walked up to her and asked what her mother's name was. She said 'Trudy Parker.' 'Course, I made it out to be lighthearted and told her she had been blessed to have such a wonderful grandmother to help out. She agreed. I quickly left because I thought I was going to pass out right there at the sound of Trudy's name.

"I didn't talk to her much after that. Just watched and listened. After what happened to Wilkerson at the church, and not knowing any reason for it, I followed you around, Detective." Hawk looked straight at Donna.

"I wanted to see if you were checking in on my little girl. But no, you had more important things to do, so I started following her everywhere to make sure she made it okay and no one harassed her." Hawk was now silent.

"*You* were the one in the pickup following me!" Donna's eyes were wide—but not as wide as Lou's, since this was all news to him.

Donna continued, "I take it Stella doesn't

227

know about you…."

"No. Why should she? I don't want her ashamed of her old man. What a coward I was to leave her mother and deprive Stella of a father. Knowing about me would just bring her more heartbreak." Hawk stared at the floor, elbows on his knees.

Lou leaned his chair back and looked at the ceiling. *How many twists and turns can possibly go on in one case? Is any of this for real? Or is God sitting somewhere on a cloud enjoying one big laugh? Somehow I've lost my sense of humor because none of this is funny anymore. We are trying to find the murderer of a murderer, and Hawk is Stella's father. Surely this is a joke. A joke, right?*

"So what did you intend to do if you caught some guy following her, Hawk?" Donna was shaken, but something told her it would turn out alright.

"I would have... well, I… I don't know. The old me would have killed him. In the beat of a heart. But, you know… it wouldn't look too good to God, and all. After giving His own son to die for me and my sins, I don't think I could just ignore that and kill someone. I don't know. I just wanted her to be safe. At least it made me feel halfway like a father. Not one she deserves, mind you, but at least a little."

Lou let his chair back down and sighed. Donna looked over at him for a long moment.

"Obviously I am going to be arrested. Can you at least tell me what law I broke?"

Lou caught the slight shake of Donna's head. He agreed, so he ran with it.

"Oh, I don't know, it's pretty bad… A father protecting his daughter…"

"Not even coming close to her property… I don't know either… pretty heavy penalty for that one." Donna was enjoying this part of it. It wasn't often they could let someone down easily.

Hawk watched them both as they spoke,

confusion all over him.

"What do you think, Lou? Probably get life with the daughter he never saw grow up.…"

"To say nothing of the probation Stella will put him on for the rest of his life!" Lou chuckled.

"Hey, wait a minute! You mean you aren't going to charge me with something?" Hawk was still not sure what he was hearing.

It was Donna who grinned and said, "Look, Hawk. You frightened Stella because she saw you following her. That was wrong. But, we are willing to overlook your shortcomings, if— and I mean *if*—you go to Stella *tomorrow* and tell her the truth. She has a right to know. And, Hawk, stop following her around!"

"*And* following my partner!" Lou got his two cents in.

"Okay. Okay…! I hope she won't be too disappointed when I tell her…." Hawk was deep in thought when the detectives stood up. He followed.

"Go home, Hawk. Get some sleep, and then arrange to meet Stella with this information."

"And don't forget...."

"Don't leave town! *I got it!*" This time Hawk was smiling as he was escorted out of the room, heading for the front door.

Once again, the partners were left in an interrogation room staring at each other. Finally, Lou shook his head.

Too tired to laugh, he smiled and said, "Girl, is any of this real? *Any* of it?"

Donna said, "No. At least not at five in the morning. Well, no need to go back home to bed. Want to get some breakfast before coming back to work?"

Lou thought that was a very good idea.

MURDER FOR A MOMENT

CHAPTER

19

Their breakfast order had been taken, and they were enjoying the coffee they both needed. The entire interview with Hawk was running through her head when Lou said something that jerked her back to reality.

"Donna, it looks like Clarissa really is carrying someone else's kid."

Donna jerked her head up to catch the

slight disappointment in his eyes.

"How do you know?"

"Well, I did what every red-blooded American boyfriend would do. I hired a Private Investigator to follow her. You remember Miles Jefferson?"

"Yes, of course. Good man. After a hundred years on the force, being a PI after retirement was perfect for him. He's very good at what he does. And he doesn't leave out a word in his reports. If a bird chirped when a car went by, he will say 'a bird chirped when a car went by.'

"I used to think that strange, but, truthfully, you never know what little detail might be important, so he's a whole lot better at reports than I am." Donna grinned at her partner.

Lou chuckled, nodded his head, and pointed back at himself, too.

"So, what did he find out?"

"Well, last Saturday he called and wanted

me to meet him, as he had information. So I met him at six, and he told me he had witnessed her talking to and being overly friendly with a black dude with a drug rap sheet."

"I'm sorry, Lou…."

"No, wait. There's more. I didn't really get into the gist of the conversation, as I wanted proof. I want pictures of them in bed together or something! The fact that she was 'overly friendly' does not make a cheater."

"No, of course not, Lou. I'm sorry…."

"No, wait. There's more!" At this point, Lou gave her a small smile. "Miles called me last night just about the time I went to bed and wanted to have dinner with me this evening to show me his proof. So, I guess there isn't any reason to think it's not real.

"Anyway, the reason I brought this up is, I would like for you to go with me tonight to meet him. You know… for some moral support, I guess." Lou was looking unhappy now.

"Of course, I will!" Donna was honored he considered her a good-enough friend to trust her with this very personal information.

"Does Clarissa know that you know?" Donna didn't want anything to happen to her partner, especially a domestic problem.

"No. She knows I have changed the locks on the doors and the security code. Boy, did I get an earful over that. I reminded her that she was the one who'd moved out and that it was my right to alter the security of my own property. She called me every kind of weasel there is for deserting my child. She threatened to raise the child to know exactly what a self-centered jackass I am." That comment brought another smile to his lips.

"I am so glad to hear about the locks and security. That was smart, Lou, and you know it." Real relief settled over Donna, remembering the money that woman took when Lou had to work.

Breakfast was served, and they ate in silence, each in their own thoughts.

~~~

The rest of the day was spent running headlong into bureaucracy and paperwork.

Lou mumbled, "...if people only knew...."

"Knew what?"

Lou looked at Donna a bit surprised but realized the point of her question.

"If people only knew the real life of a police detective. People seem to think it is glamorous, but it really is mostly mundane and repetitious." He closed one folder, dropped it on a pile and grabbed another one.

Donna just smiled. "You have to admit, we would make a really boring television show."

A moment later she added, "Lou, I am a little concerned about Tracy. She hasn't called me back."

"Put a BOLO out on her if you want." Lou smiled at her. He knew there were many reasons why Tracy might not have called back.

"Very funny! No, I'm not ready for that, but I wonder why I haven't heard from her. I just want a couple of answers about the day Wilkerson died, and she said she was feeling ill."

"I know, but don't worry until there is something to worry about. Gads, I sound like you, now! Heaven help me!" He didn't duck fast enough to miss the pencil headed for him.

Donna's phone rang. Upon answering she was bombarded with a bubbly Stella.

"I found my father! You knew it! He told me so. Can you believe it? I have a father!"

Stella was going a mile a minute so Donna just listened with a smile.

"He told me what happened way back then. I can't say I blame him... what with all he had to endure as a boy. I know my mother never looked for another man so he must have been special! Can you believe it?"

Finally given a chance to respond, Donna said, "I am happy for you, Stella. You deserve answers and I am pleased we were able to find some for you. Plus, you no longer have to worry about being followed. You both have so much to talk about and that will take time."

"I know!" Stella said. "We are having dinner to go over some more stuff. I can't wait. Thank you again for everything."

After saying their goodbyes, Donna relayed the happy news to Lou. They chuckled about the unbelievable outcome before getting back to work.

By five that evening, both were exhausted. The lack of sleep was written all over them. The captain noticed and told them both not to show up the next day until noon. Neither one of them argued.

Leaving, Lou said he would follow her home and then they would go together in his car.

The meeting with Miles was set for the Red Rock Canyon Grill on North Rock Road. It was one of Donna's favorite places, so she perked up a bit.

After parking her car at her condo, she got into Lou's Mercedes, and they headed north. The restaurant was already packed, but with reservations they were quickly seated.

Within minutes, they were joined by Miles. Donna had forgotten just how handsome the man was, even in his late fifties. Sitting at the table with him and Lou made her the envy of the place! She smiled to herself at that.

"Miles, you remember my partner, Donna Decker?" Lou was taking control.

"Of course, I remember Donna. I'm not blind, Lou. Hey, pretty lady, remember that party when the waiter got drunk, and all that food fell to the floor?" He laughed with Donna as they threw out memories of the night in question.

"No kidding!" Donna remarked. "Can

you believe that? He kept mumbling something to himself about surfing, I think."

"Yeah," Miles said, "he was singing, or at least trying to sing one of the Beach Boys' old songs! I laughed 'til the tears came that night."

"Me, too!" Donna and Miles laughed out loud.

Lou was left in the dark as to how long these two must have known each other. *Is Miles an old boyfriend? No, surely not! Miles is twenty years her senior. And married! Still....* He didn't like the thought. *They do make a great-looking couple...*

"All right you guys, so much for reminiscing...," Lou wanted to get away from the thought of men in Donna's life. He didn't know why, but it irritated him.

"How's Jefferson Investigations going for you, Miles?" Donna smiled sweetly at the man sitting next to her. Across the table she could see how uncomfortable Lou felt, and it tickled her.

241

"Never better, sweetheart. Oh, if there were just three more of me, I would be rich beyond my…."

"Hey, guys!" It was Lou. "Let's have dinner!" Both of his friends laughed at him, but they turned back to the menus.

More than an hour later, they were enjoying a latte after a great dinner and lots of fun conversation. Now it was time for the not-so-fun stuff.

Miles looked at Lou and said, "It's obvious you wanted Donna to know what is going on, or you wouldn't have brought her. If it's alright with you, I will bring her up to date on what I have been doing, and then we'll go out to my car for the rest." Lou nodded, and Miles turned to Donna.

"Here's the scoop. I was hired by Lou to follow his girlfriend, Clarissa. Seems she is pregnant and says it's his kid. He wants to know her every activity. I have known Lou for years, and I have the highest respect for the WPD., since I was one of their finest, so I cut him a really discounted price. He didn't want me to, but I figured if I just make my expenses, we're both good."

Both men looked at each other with admiration and respect. Then Lou said, "He's just trying to make me think I owe him one!"

Everyone chuckled when Miles raised his eyebrows and said to Donna, "He does. Boy, does he ever!"

Then Miles continued bringing her up to date, "It didn't take me long to find a whole bunch of stuff. Every night, she would drive by Lou's place—I guess just to make sure he was home—and then off she would go to some bar or restaurant to meet this guy named Lloyd Buchannan. He is a tall, nice-looking African-American male. I got a couple of pictures of them together on my camera.

"But, ever the detective, Lou wanted proof—like pictures of them weren't enough. Okay, so I back-track and start over.

"Now, it's one thing to have dinner or a drink with someone, but was this relationship any more than friends? That didn't take long either. They went to dinner and sat at a corner table. I called one of my female employees to meet there as my 'date' so we could get close. Not as pretty as you, Donna, but she's really good at helping me." Miles smiled at a beaming Donna.

Miles continued, "When she arrived, I requested the table next to theirs, pretending it was so my girl and I could have privacy. We acted the part, and Clarissa and Lloyd hardly noticed us. I placed a recording device that looked like a cigarette lighter on the table. Since it was a no-smoking place, I was taking a chance, but they didn't even notice.

"They had already ordered, so we got ordered and waited. I asked my 'date' the usual questions. 'How was your day, honey?' Stuff like that, in a quiet voice, and she answered the same way. The corner area was indeed private and quiet.

"That's when it was all caught for the

record." Miles swung a sad look to Lou, knowing it would not be easy for him to hear everything his ex-girlfriend had said.

Steeling himself, Lou said, "Okay, let's get out of here and go listen to Clarissa making a fool out of me." He dropped a hundred-dollar bill on the table to pay the tab.

Donna put her arm through his, and they walked out together. Miles was driving one of his many vehicles, and, tonight it was an older Cadillac. It was the perfect car to have in some poorer neighborhoods and watch people. It wouldn't be out of place.

Lou got into the front seat, next to Miles, and Donna jumped into the back seat, not wanting to get in the way.

Miles started the player, laid it on the dash, and they all listened.

It was the boyfriend, Lloyd, who started off with a question.

"How are we going to make him think it's his kid? Can you tell me that? He said he is going to wait until the DNA test was taken, so you know he's going to find out it's not his. He won't know it's mine, but he'll sure know it ain't his."

Clarissa blew his concerns right off. "Don't worry so much, baby. He is going to marry me before the kid is born. Then there is nothing he can do. He will be the legal father."

"And what makes you think he is going to marry you sooner? He hasn't fallen for that yet."

"Because I know him, baby. He can't resist me. I am going to threaten to leave Wichita with his kid and let some other man raise it! That will put the end to all his stupid stuff. He'll agree to marriage right away just to keep me in town. It's just that witch of a

mother he has who's causing all of this, anyway. She thinks she is so much better than I am, with her money and all. But I can tell you one thing; I'm smarter than she is. You can bet on that! Once I have that mommas boy in my pocket, she won't know what hit her. You and I will live like kings on their money. 'Course we will have to hide our relationship for a little while, but not for long. He is so busy working all the time with that slut of a partner that he can't see what is going on right under his nose."

"Sounds good, girl. I would sure love to quit being a janitor. Manual labor is not my thing."

"I know what your 'thing' is, baby. Let's blow this place and get on with the hanky-panky. You owe me a good time tonight, baby."

247

Miles turned to the back seat and addressed Donna, "Well, like I said, I got it all on tape. I have seen gold-diggers in my time, but this one takes the cake."

Lou had his face in his hands, not saying anything. Donna's heart went out to him, but she knew there was nothing she could do.

It was quiet in the car for a few more minutes. When Lou raised his face, Donna's heart broke to see the tears. He turned to exit the car, and she quietly did the same to follow him to his car.

The ride back to her place was quiet. Donna wanted to throttle Clarissa for doing this to a good man like Lou. At least he'd found out before it had taken an even worse toll.

Before getting out of his car, she leaned over and kissed his cheek. As gently as she could, she said, "She's the one who lost tonight, Lou. Not you."

She left him with a look of surprise and wonder on his face.

CHAPTER

20

It was about a week after Donna had spoken with Cassie about Jacqueline's case being reopened as a homicide. The next-door neighbor at the apartment complex stated they, too, had seen Wilkerson coming out of her apartment that fateful day. Not being able to prove the crime didn't mean it didn't happen that way.

Still open? Yes. Solved? Yes. The fact

that Jackie had not committed suicide would not bring her back, but at least they know she hadn't given up. She'd been murdered.

So it was a bit of a surprise when Donna saw Cassie walking toward her desk. A uniform had pointed Donna's desk area out, and Cassie was walking toward her, tears falling down her face. She was holding something near her chest.

Donna jumped up to meet her, horrified at the pain on the woman's face. Cassie then held both hands out toward her. In one hand she was holding a book.

"After you told me she didn't kill herself, I decided to go through her things in my basement…," Cassie was one-half inch above hysterics, so Donna was holding her hands and the book all at the same time.

"I found this book… her journal… it explains everything. Why didn't she tell me? I could have helped her! Why?" With that, Cassie collapsed crying to the floor.

Donna asked anyone around her for some

water, and she knelt beside the distraught woman.

"Jackie was an incredible woman, Cassie. You should be very proud of her. She went through hell and came out the other end. She didn't let the likes of Wilkerson intimidate her; she fought back." Donna's heart broke for Cassie.

"But, it was *her* fight, Cassie. Don't blame yourself. It was something she felt she had to do alone." Donna held Cassie's head and let her sip the water. Someone handed her a wet washcloth, and she held it on Cassie's head. Within a couple of minutes, the woman was able to sit up and then stand.

"I am so sor…."

"Don't even go there, Cassie. I would feel the same if it had been my sister. I am just grateful The Man Upstairs allowed us to find out the truth. I will read her words carefully, I promise."

"Take your time. Really. It's hard to rush through that ugliness, but when you are through…."

Donna nodded their silent agreement to return Jackie's voice on paper. She walked Cassie out of the precinct to the elevators. They said their goodbyes after a hug.

When Donna re-entered, everyone stopped what they were doing to look at her. She was just about to tear someone's eyes out when the captain stepped out of his office.

"*What?* You've never seen a heartbroken woman before? Get back to *work*!"

She nodded at him as she returned to her desk. His bellow was much more effective than hers would have been.

Lou's saddened face nodded at her, too, as he stared at the book. He left her to the task at hand but closely watched her face to see if she was about to break down.

Cassie was right about one thing. It was not pretty reading. The hurt, fear, and then anger she felt at being raped. Then the rapist goes free. But that was not the end of her anguish. She found out she was pregnant. She had terrible morning sickness for several months as she waited for the birth. From her religious upbringing, she knew she couldn't have an abortion, for any reason, but that didn't mean she had to raise the child.

But what Donna found out about this woman wasn't so much how angry she was, but how accepting she was. Oh, she wanted the man to pay for what he had done, so he couldn't do it to anyone else, but she didn't completely blame him. She blamed herself for working in the bar in the first place. What victim would do that?

"If Mom and Dad only knew how I was spending my time. Partying almost every day, drinking along with the crowd, living in the darkness of a nightclub. I know that is why I stay so far away from Houston because I don't want to embarrass them. Why do I do it?

253

Why? I don't know. It's like I don't know anything else. I just don't know how to live a normal life. That has got to change...."

"I have a baby on the way, and my first welfare check is coming in a few days, along with food stamps. How I hate that. I have always paid my own way, and now I can't even put food in my own body for a baby. "The police think I am a whore and, apparently, the man who raped me does, too. Am I? Because I was not a virgin, does that make me a whore? Well, no more. I will never live the night life again. If it was God wanting to get my attention, it worked. I'm sorry, God. Forgive me. I promise I will change my life."

"I felt the baby kick today—more than once. I am about four and a half months along. Doc says I am going to have a girl. The sonogram showed her. Almost seems wrong for

a rapist to have a little girl. Thankfully, he won't be raising her. Man, how time drags. I really feel this is a test from God. My payment for my sins, so to speak. I have nothing to do all day but wait. Wait to be five months pregnant. Wait to be six months... I read the Bible a lot, trying to find answers, I guess. But He knows my heart. I will turn my life around. He'll see."

"Six months along, and the adoption papers have been dealt with. I wonder who will raise my child, my little girl. I wonder what she will look like. No, I can't go there. The thought she would look like 'him' frightens me. I will get a little money to start life over again. At least I won't have to worry about how to get home. I just want to hug my Mom. It is times like this that a girl thinks of her Mom. Only a mother would understand what I am

going through. Dad's thoughts would be totally different. Ha, the thought almost brings a smile."

"Well, seven months now. I am bored out of my mind. I feel like I have read more books than the library carries. Some good, some not so good, but it passes the days away. Boy, am I getting big. She kicks and moves around a lot now. I wish I knew what her name was going to be so I could think of her by name. Lord, please give her a happy home because I sure can't.

"My stomach is huge. I understand the term 'beached whale' now. It's true. That's what I look like. Eight months along, and I can't wait to have this over. Enough already. Okay, it's not the little girl's fault, Lord. I know that. Sorry for my impatience. Make sure she finds a good home."

"Well, here I am, finally in the

hospital. I am told I had a healthy child. That's good. I pray the new parents are wonderful to her like mine were to me. The sad thing is I will miss her… always. She is in your hands now, Lord. I can't do any more for her."

"Life isn't going as well as I had hoped. I think about my baby all day. What does she look like? Is she happy? What is her name? Is she right handed or left handed? Did good people get her? Will I ever see her again? How am I supposed to start a new life, Lord, when I am tortured by the past one?"

"Time to get out of here. I never want to see Kansas City again. All of my wandering fever is gone. I just want to go home and spend time with my parents. How can I face them knowing they are grandparents but will never see her? Lord, will my

life get easier now? I have tried to do the right thing. Now I just want to go home."

Donna read for the rest of the day but only got to the part where she gave up the child for adoption and wanted nothing more than to go home and see her Mom and Dad.

Packing up the book, she declined a detective's offer to meet a group for a drink. Donna told them she had research to do. It was true. This was research… *painful* research. Lou went out with them, knowing how she was going to spend her evening. He was going to read it after she finished.

Donna stopped at Dillon's Supermarket for their great takeout Chinese and headed home. Once there, she showered, put on comfy lounge clothes, and curled up with a TV tray of food and the journal.

Donna cried when she read about the death of Jackie's parents. What daughter wouldn't? She couldn't begin to imagine the pain… but it was the sentiment in the journal that struck Donna.

"I love being home with my parents, and they seem to be happy to see me. I wonder if my little girl looks like me or my mother? I hope she will be just as sweet as Mom is. As you know, Lord, I am going to church with them. Being close to you is the only thing that is keeping me together."

"I can't really believe they are gone. They were just here, for God's sake! God? God, were you in on this, too? Did you send me home because you knew their time was about up? I feel so grateful for having had some time to spend with them before they were killed! You are guiding my life, Lord. I just pray it is to a good place."

Donna stopped and laid down the book. She could do nothing at this point but say a prayer of her own: "Heavenly Father, I don't know how she was able to see your hand in some of the things most people would think terrible, but you were guiding her back to you. She prayed that you were guiding her to a good place, and we know there is no greater place than Heaven."

All of her emotions had been drained from her today. It was time to stop. She would take up the journal again tomorrow morning.

She called Lou and brought him up to date on what she had read. She told him he could read it for himself the following day. Neither one of them could grasp the terrible truth about the pregnancy.

When she finished, Lou had news for her, too. Seems he had his attorney write a letter to Clarissa. Not only was it hand delivered, but Miles wanted the pleasure of delivering it. himself. Lou said the letter explained that he knew of her scheme to defraud him and his mother out of money; knew the unborn child was not his, despite her lies; knew of her lover, the baby's father; and could prove it all because it was caught on tape and in photos. Therefore, if she was ever seen near him, or his mother, or their homes again, he would have her arrested and charged with all of the "above."

Miles told Lou she turned very pale when she read it. The fear on her face was real, and he didn't think she would be bothering Lou again. Donna couldn't think of any better news and thanked Lou for sharing. She said she needed something to pick her spirits up.

Now, it was time for bed. Donna slept soundly for the first time in ages.

After putting the large mug of coffee on her desk the next morning, she sat and opened the journal again.

> *"Cassie asked me to move back with her to Wichita. She said I am the only sister she had (our two brothers don't count because they are guys!) and would love to be*

261

able to see me on a regular basis. She also said since she is in the TV biz, maybe she could get me a related job. How cool would that be, God? I think it is the place for me right now. Time to pack."

"I really like the Jimmy Swaggart stuff on the radio, Lord. It's special to me. I know that preacher is Your messenger! Where can I find a church that preaches that same message? I know Cassie doesn't go to church any more, but maybe I can convince her...."

"Hey, Lord! I called the Jimmy Swaggart phone number, and they told me about the one church here in Wichita. I will go next Sunday! Yaaaay!"

"Lord, you know what I am going to say. He was there. At church. HE was there. Why? Why did you lead me right to the man who hurt me so badly? What have I done

that I deserve this? Have I not been through enough? Is there more anguish I have to endure before I am free?"

"He smirks at me when he can catch my eye. I have to find a way to talk to his wife and let her know what he really is. I have to tell her! She certainly doesn't know what kind of man he is!"

And then Donna saw the last entry:

"I've seen him following me. Oh Lord, I am so afraid. Please help me find a safe place!"

Donna dropped the journal in front of Lou, left her desk, and went to the ladies room to let the tears fall. It wouldn't do for the guys out there to see weakness in someone who might be needed to have their six. In her mind she said, *Thank you Lord, for giving her Heaven forever.*

There's no safer place than that.

She recouped and returned to her desk to find Miles Jefferson standing there. Thinking it was about Lou, she started to step away when Lou said, "Stay—this involves you, too."

CHAPTER

21

Miles Jefferson said, "It's about the Wilkerson case!"

Lou gave Donna a shrug, and the three of them went into interview room two. Miles didn't wait for any questions. He had been in and around this business long enough to know what he had to do. After the recorder was clicked on, each party identified themselves, and then he started.

"I was hired by Mrs. Caroline Wilkerson, in late August of this year, to find out the parents of her adopted child. She told me the birth date and place — Kansas City, Kansas, plus the attorney's name she'd used to make it all legal. Her concern was for the baby's health. She'd had one baby die of crib death—her *own* baby, mind you. So she was adamant about keeping her adopted girl safe. You have to admire a lady like that. It's one of those cases you actually enjoy doing 'cause the end result was for the good of someone. At least that was what I thought at the time."

Miles made himself more comfortable; then he continued.

"I told her it would be expensive because adoptions are as private as they get. She said she understood and gave me a ten-thousand dollar retainer. Cash, mind you. I said, 'Okay, I'm headed for Kansas City.'

"First trip was pretty much what I expected. No one could tell me anything. I met with a K.C.P.D. friend for lunch; he will remain anonymous, but I'll call him Derrick. I asked for his help. He was pretty skeptical about what he could do for me, but we'd had each other's backs over the years, so he said he would try. I told him that's all I could expect from him. He's a good guy. I knew he would do what he could.

"I didn't want to leave him without leverage, if you know what I mean, so I gave him twenty-five hundred bucks for starters, in case some wheels needed greasing, you know? He appreciated it. That way he wouldn't have to use his own dough and bill me later. It works out for both of us.

"I returned to Wichita and waited. Daily, I kept thinking I would hear something. I was getting a little nervous about the silence, but, after a week went by, I got a call. It was Derrick. He said the money had come in handy because a receptionist for the adopting attorney was in dire straits.

"Seems her boyfriend owed a drug dealer a couple grand, and things were getting desperate. She didn't hesitate at all. She said that, for two grand, she would copy every file the attorney had! Boy, would that guy ever been pissed if he found out.

"Didn't need them all, of course, just the one for Caroline and Henry Wilkerson. Derrick said he should have it by the end of the next week.

"Another week went by, and I didn't hear anything. I was getting calls from my client, so I buzzed Derrick at home one night.

"Miles," he said, "I was just gonna call you." Yeah, okay—so I asked what he had. He said that Caroline and Henry Wilkerson hadn't adopted the baby. I said, 'What are you talking about? Of course, they did. I saw the kid myself.' I was shocked and wondering if my old buddy was on something.

"No, Derrick said only Caroline did! Henry wasn't there and didn't sign for it or anything. In fact, she claimed she was a wealthy widow and wanted to adopt a little girl in a certain age range. Seems she was looking for a child about the same age as the baby she'd lost.

Kinda creepy, don't 'cha think? Especially since she really is a wealthy widow *now*."

Miles stopped for a drink of water before going on.

"Anyway, he said that's all he had right then. He had the name of the mother and was trying to locate her. I asked him if he wanted me back up there and he said maybe later.

"I let the client know I had a lead on the mother and would get back to her when I could.

"Next I heard from Derrick, he was all excited. He says the adoption was the result of an S.V.U. case that was still open. It had been four years then, and it was still open! Can you believe that?

"Anyway, he said he was trying to get info out of their computer but didn't have access. He said he was going to need a lot more money. At this point I told him I didn't want to know anything else about what he was doing. He knew if he did something illegal and I knew about it, I would have to turn him in. It would be the same with me, if he knew. So he said, 'Yeah, okay.' I told him I would be up on Monday.

"I told the client I had a lead on the mother of the child but needed more money to follow it through. She didn't hesitate to give me ten-thousand more in cash. Some people just have all the money they need, I guess.

"Early Monday morning, I drove north and met with Derrick around eleven for coffee. I asked him how much he needed and he said five thousand would do. So, I handed over the cash. Derrick said he didn't think it was a domestic-abuse case from what he could tell. He told me to check into the hotel across the street and that he would see me after work this evening.

"He said he couldn't have dinner with me that night because he needed to get home to his wife and kids. Guess she had been complaining 'cause work kept him out so much. I could understand that. The one thing he knew right then was the mother's name. It was Jacqueline Marie Harpcr. I rolled that around for a while after Derrick left."

Donna jumped up, knocking her chair backwards against the wall. *"Jackie Harper! You're kidding me! You! Are! Kidding! Me! Jackie's baby is the one Caroline adopted?"*

Lou was too stunned to talk. He stared at the wall. This case was one of the worst he had ever worked.

Miles smiled and continued, "I take it you know Ms. Harper, then? Oh, hang in there, it only gets better. So I trotted over to the hospital where the kid had been born. I am not going to tell you how I obtained the information, and I am sure it is your stand that you don't want to know. Is that right?"

Lou and Donna looked at each other and both shook their heads "No." Miles flashed a smile as they all understood that, if Miles had done anything illegal, they would have to report it, just like the K.C. cop. So, not knowing such a thing, there was nothing to report.

"Don't know the dude's name, but he was one of those employees who worked in the

271

office where the files were kept. I told him we were looking into an old case where a lady had put a kid up for adoption, but the case was still open. I told him we wanted to make sure the lady still wanted to press charges, but the address we had for her was no longer any good. Could he help?

"Jackie Harper said she was in a bar one evening when this man kept following her around. She described him in detail, even the man's name. Sometime during the night, she claims she was drugged and didn't remember anything until the following morning. Sounds like the date-rape drug to me. When she woke up, she was in his bed at his hotel, and he was in the shower.

"She was petrified and quickly got dressed and left the room. She called police, and they all arrived back at the guy's room. When he opened the door, he acted like he and Jackie were long-time lovers and couldn't understand why she would make such silly accusations.

"Here's where you will love this. The guy's name was Henry Wilkerson! Yep, our boy

Henry. She was furious and wanted him arrested, but they didn't have any cause. It was 'he said, she said.'

"The staff at the bar where she worked was questioned, but all anyone could remember was him following her around. Were they a couple? They didn't know. They spoke to each other from time to time, but the bar was too crowded to really make sense of anything. The bartender said Henry bought her a couple of drinks; so, yeah, he could have put something in one of them, but he didn't see anything.

"So the case went cold, and no one was actually arrested. Only the accusation hung out there. It must have been quite a shock when you are trying to get on with your life and then find out you're pregnant. Man, if that had been my daughter, I'm not sure what I would have done to the creep.

"Anyway, seems she stayed in Kansas City until the baby was born, but moved to a small apartment on the Kansas side. Guess she wanted to be away from where it had happened. That's why the cops couldn't find her, since she'd actually left Missouri. After the baby was born, she left Kansas. She didn't say where she was going, but she did say where she was from. So that was a place to start.

"I found her brother, Mason, in Houston, but he definitely didn't want to talk about Jackie. He wouldn't tell me where she was or anything. He was downright angry that I would ask. All he would say is she'd gone to Kansas. Really? But she just came from there.

"Or was it another place in Kansas, like Wichita? Wouldn't it be funny if she was sitting in Wichita all this time and didn't know her child had been adopted in Wichita? Oh, well. Time to go back."

Donna spoke up, "So you are the one who talked to Mason first! I should have known. He hinted I wasn't the first to ask Jackie's whereabouts. I felt bad about bothering him because he sure didn't want to talk about her."

"Yeah, that's the attitude I got from him,

too—in spades!" Miles chuckled after his remark.

"So, back at home. I searched for the name and came up with only a sister, Cassie. I recognized the name. I'd seen Cassie Harper on TV now and then. So I put in a call to her. Of course, I couldn't tell her why I was calling but just that I wanted to speak with Jackie. Did she know where she was?

"There is no doubt Cassie was stunned by my request, but not nearly as stunned as I was when she told me Jackie had committed suicide about a year before. She didn't have any idea why. I thanked her for her kindness and hung up.

"Now what? I mean, what am I going to tell my client? So, anyway, I went digging into deaths in the Wichita area from one to two years back, and I found her. The *Wichita Eagle* had run an obit on her with a picture. Boy, she was a looker, and so young, just twenty-three. What a waste.

"Now, I had a picture of a bit of her life.

She was working in a bar in Kansas City, Missouri. She got raped, and no one would do anything about it. Then she found out she was pregnant. She gave her baby up for adoption and went back home. Then, her parents were both killed! Gads, I mean, what else can happen to this poor girl? Right?

"She went to Wichita to live near her only sister and start a new life. But, for whatever, reason, moving to a new place didn't work out for her and she decided she couldn't go on.

"I have a friend who works for the utility company, and I had him check back then where her account was. Seemed she lived in an apartment complex in the Twin Lakes Apt. complex. I went to the complex manager and asked her about her.

"Well the woman seemed broken up about it still. Apparently Jackie had been well liked. I asked if her neighbors were still the same ones who'd lived there at the time of Jackie's death. She told me the neighbors to the north of Jackic's apartment were the same folks, the Clarks. I thanked her and left.

"When I knocked on the Clark's door, I heard a child yell, 'Mom! Someone's at the door!'

"When a woman answered, I asked if she was Mrs. Clark, and she confirmed she was. I asked her about Jackie and if she knew of anything that might have caused her to want to die. She didn't know of anything. She even seemed to have a man in her life.

"Well, she had my attention at that point, if you know what I mean. By now I knew she had been raped by Wilkerson and had given birth to his child. Then she found herself living in the same city that he lived in. Could she have run into him somewhere?

"I pulled up a picture of Wilkerson on my phone and asked her if this was the man. It sure was, she said. She said she had seen him come and go from the apartment a couple of times toward the end. I thanked Mrs. Clark and left.

"So, Jackie went to live in Wichita to be near her sister and ran smack dab into her rapist.

277

There was no getting away from him here. Memories she can't bear to live with were haunting her. She figured the only way to be rid of him was to kill herself.

"Now, here's where I went sideways. It had been a little over four weeks since I'd started on this case. I now had all the information my client wanted. But keep in mind that this was about two weeks ago, in late September, when all of this info finally came together, Wilkerson was still alive and was living with my client. I was really concerned about her finding out.

"What if she said something to him and he killed her? I mean, rape and murder aren't too far apart. So I kept stalling. I told her I had this piece of info here and that one there and that I would get it to her.

"When Wilkerson was found dead, obviously, the first thing I think of is my client! She had motive—but she didn't know it. It was a tough spot to be in, so I waited a week or so to give you guys some time to check things out.

"So, when Mrs. Wilkerson wasn't

arrested, I wrote up my report. I hated to have to let her know all of this, especially since she'd just became a widow, but it is information she'd paid handsomely for. When I gave it to her, I informed her it was not pretty.

"I also told her I would have to turn over this same report to the police because of the Jackie Harper case being reopened. It definitely had information the police would want. She had no problem with that before she even read it. She really is a nice lady.

"The end, detectives. That's all I know." Miles let the words fall where they may.

The three of them spent the next hour going over particulars and explaining to Miles how they'd found out Wilkerson had killed her, that she hadn't died by her own hand.

"I wish I could have been the one who killed that filthy rag…" Miles mumbled as he left them at the table and walked out.

In their business, goodbyes were not

necessary. Miles left the detectives with a lot to think about.

After several minutes of silence, Lou looked at Donna and said, "I won't even apologize for my feelings, but I wish I could have put a bullet between his eyes."

CHAPTER

22

After Miles left, they returned to their desks to go over his report for any detail they may not have known or missed. At least they knew now who'd beat them to asking the questions. The investigator's report just substantiated what they already knew. And now Caroline knew it, too.

Suddenly they heard, "Lou, Donna! You have *got* to see this!"

Donna jumped, "What is it?" She watched as Detective Kent Walker came rushing up to them.

"We have your perp—on film, no less! We got them!"

Donna was pretty sure she stopped breathing. She looked over at Lou, and he looked like he didn't even want to know. They were led into the room with the TV and DVD player. One of the detectives, Stan Berkley, was smiling at them like he had just won the lottery. If this film showed them Wilkerson's killer, then it might just be the lottery.

"You guys went over the surveillance tapes last week. Why are you finding something now?" Lou was just as confused as she was.

"Give us a break, McGregor. We started with every camera we found in either direction from the church. This one is over a mile from the church. We just got to it this morning. Sheez, man."

Donna just wanted to see it. "You are

both grounded if you don't shut up and show me this film."

The light went off, and the film popped up on the screen. What they could see were people walking in and out of a building. The time on it stated it was in the morning hours, about three-thirty. Donna started to ask what this place was when Lou spoke up.

"Is that a QuickTrip?"

Stan nodded, "Yep. The one on South Seneca, about a mile north of the church."

She saw nothing of interest and was getting annoyed when something caught her eye. The pay phone. Someone was at the pay phone, and they looked familiar.

Stan was watching their faces for reactions "Look familiar? I can go in closer."

He zoomed in on the person standing at the pay phone, and there was no denying it was Tracy Andrews, Caroline's sister. She said she had been ill and was home in bed, but there she was, a mile from the murder scene, making a phone call.

"We called the phone company and got a report on that phone. It was to a cab company. After reaching *them*, I called the dude who picked her up.. Today is his day off, and he should be here any moment." Walker left the room to check on the cabby.

Lou and Donna stared at the picture on the screen and hated what they saw. Caroline had been through so much, and now she would find out her sister had killed her husband. Or had it been Caroline's idea? Could it have been a conspiracy? At least it had been narrowed down to….

"Here he is! This is Gus Zether. Gus, sit right here." Walker came in with a short, stocky man with a friendly smile.

For the next 30 minutes, they questioned Zether about the woman he'd picked up at the Q.T. on the night in question. He remembered her because of her looks. She told him she had car trouble. His records showed he took her to the Twin Lakes Apartments.

They thanked him for coming in and showed the man out.

Donna and Lou went back to their desks, stunned but excited at the same time. The captain was getting the arrest warrant, and they were going to go pick up Tracy. While waiting for the paperwork, they tried to figure out how it all had gone down, but nothing made sense.

"From what she said, she disliked the man so much she wouldn't even be in the same room alone with him. How in the...?" Lou was throwing bits and pieces out.

"I don't have a clue. But I have to tell you, I sure don't like it." Donna didn't want to have to arrest anyone for the murder, really, but especially anyone from the family that he had so badly abused.

They grabbed the arrest warrant from the captain and headed for the door. That's when they saw her. Tracy. She walked in the door with her sister, Caroline.

"I've come to turn myself in. But first, I want to talk to you guys." Tracy nodded at Lou and Donna.

Donna took her arm and showed Tracy the direction of the interrogation room, then followed her in. Caroline sat down next to her. It was obvious she was there for moral support.

Donna hooked up the recorder and had everyone identify themselves for the record. Caroline was allowed to stay under the stipulation she didn't say a word during the interview. She agreed, and the two held hands. Tracy would rub Caroline's hand if she was having a hard time.

Lou started first, to get the preliminaries over with.

"Tracy Lynn Anderson, you have the right to remain silent. Anything you say can and will be used against you in a court of law. You have the right to an attorney. If you cannot afford an attorney, one will be provided for you.

"Do you understand?" Lou looked right at her.

"Yes."

"Do you want an attorney present?"

"No."

"Have you been forced in any way, by anyone, into making this statement?"

"No."

"Sign this statement to that fact. You are giving up your right to have an attorney present."

Lou gathered the signed paper and sat at one end of the table; Donna was across from Tracy and Caroline. She looked at Tracy and said, "Tell us what happened."

Tracy sat upright, took a deep breath, and then looked into her sister's eyes with love and sadness. She looked at Lou and then at Donna. That's when she started talking.

"I might as well start from the beginning because that is where my nightmare started. I met Henry five years ago when my sister, Caroline, married him. It was a month after I had moved to Wichita to be closer to her. He seemed nice and certainly capable of giving her a nice lifestyle.

"They had been married for six months when he knocked on my apartment door. I was surprised to see him, but not alarmed. He said Caroline had some ladies' meeting, and he thought we could go get a bite to eat. That sounded fine, so we went to a local steak house for dinner and then back to my apartment.

"He brought in a bottle of wine, and said he would like to end the evening the right way, with a glass of Domaine Cru. Actually the wines real name is Domaine Ramonet Montrachet Grand Cru Chardonnay. Yeah, I know ridiculously long name but that stuff is worth more than $1,000 a bottle—several thousand in some places!

"I couldn't believe it! So yes, I was thrilled to have a glass of that wine with him. The only way I knew about that high-end stuff was because my girlfriend in college got married to a stockbroker, and that wine had been served at their wedding! I loved it, but not enough to pay that price.

"Henry went into the kitchen, and he seemed to be there a little longer than I thought it should have taken, but, again, I wasn't concerned. He was, after all, my brother-in-law. When he walked into the living room with two glasses, he handed me one and kept the other. He sat across the room from me, so it wasn't like he was crowding me or anything. I felt comfortable at that time.

"The wine was delicious, so it didn't take me long to finish the glass. A few minutes later, I started feeling dizzy. My mind wasn't thinking right. One glass of wine doesn't make you like this, so I couldn't figure out what was going on. Henry came up to me all concerned and asked if he could help. He said he would lay me down on my bed and leave. That's the last I remember until morning.

"I awoke with no clothes on, and I had been raped. I was mortified! This was my sister's husband! She had just married him and was so in love! Part of me couldn't believe it was him and the other part knew it was. I didn't tell anyone, let alone Caroline. I just couldn't break her heart. That had already been done once before when she lost her first husband overseas.

"When I saw him after that, he acted like nothing had happened. He was just his usual courteous self. It made me fume inside, but I couldn't say anything in front of Caroline. On one occasion, when she left to go to the liquor store for more dinner wine, I told him what a pig he was for what he'd done to me.

"You know what he said? He said, as he remembered it, I had thrown myself at him, and, when he wanted to leave, I bared my breasts to entice him to stay… at least that is what he would tell Caroline if she ever found out. I was stunned. I was the innocent victim, and he had it all set up so that I would be the villain if I said one word.

"My hatred for him remained, but nothing more happened over the next two years. During that time, Caroline became pregnant and gave birth to Cathleen. I loved that baby almost as much as Caroline did. She was so beautiful and sweet. A quiet baby if you can believe that.

"Caroline had told me about the way Henry had treated her since she got pregnant. Him being a scumbag didn't surprise me a bit. He didn't want the father image—that's for sure.

"My sister had been extremely happy when she found out she was pregnant with Cathleen. A baby would be the perfect touch to their lives—a precious little thing who would love her whether her hair was fixed or not.

"Much to her shock and dismay, those sentiments were not shared by Henry. He was horrified. He wanted her to get an abortion. A child did not fit into his lifestyle.

"'Do you have any idea what that will do to my image, let alone your figure?' He said things like that! He was especially angry when she refused to terminate the pregnancy.

"That is when her marriage ended. She said he never touched her again and showed only disgust when her belly grew ever larger. The last few months before the baby was born, he stopped taking her with him to meetings and parties. He said she looked hideous.

"She did everything she could to please him. Her hair, nails, skin all got extra attention so he would be pleased. She worked out with small weights to make sure the extra weight didn't cause flab. Though she looked wonderful to everyone else, she never knew it because Henry couldn't bear to look at her.

"The rejection hit Caroline hard. But in her heart, she felt he would come around when he saw the beautiful child they had made together.

"When Cathleen was born, Henry was not at the hospital, nor did he come to visit. His life went on as normal while she gave birth to another human being. I was the one who was with her. I was the one who brought her home from the hospital with the baby. And I was the one who stayed for two days while she got back on her feet. Henry was gone on one of his business trips. He had never acknowledged any of her messages on his cell or home phone.

"He refused to have anything to do with her or the child. Caroline begged and pleaded for him to care for his own daughter, but nothing would get through to him, and she stopped trying. He never held his daughter, and he left the room if Caroline came in carrying her.

"Cathleen was five months old when I was babysitting her while Caroline went shopping. We were enjoying spending time with each other because Henry was out of town for a few days again. It was always nicer when he wasn't there.

"The baby was asleep upstairs when I heard a noise that didn't make sense coming from her room. I ran up there, and I saw Henry holding a pillow over her face! I screamed and knocked into him, trying to get him off her, but it was no use. She was so tiny, she didn't have a chance.

"Henry murdered Cathleen. He murdered his own baby."

CHAPTER

23

Donna immediately stopped the recorder, looking at Caroline. "You knew about that *when?*"

Tears welled in her eyes and said, "I just learned about it two days ago. Tracy has been staying at my place, spending time telling me all the horror that had occurred that I didn't know about. She didn't know about your calls because she'd shut her phone off so she would not be disturbed by anyone while she did her best to tell me the painful truth.

"Heddy did a wonderful job of taking care of Shana while we talked and cried and talked some more." Caroline let the tears fall. There was no reason not to.

Donna said, "Okay," turned the recorder back on, and nodded at Tracy.

"When I saw he had killed the baby, I was hysterical and screaming at him. I told him I was going to call the police and tell them what he had done. I told him I was going to make sure he died in prison!

"He doubled up his fist and hit me right in the stomach. I doubled over with the pain and fell to the floor. For a second, I thought I would be next to die. He said he would have punched my stupid face in, but he wasn't about to leave any marks on me that anyone could see.

"I was still on the floor when he knelt down and told me what I was going to do. I was to wait about two hours and then check on the baby. When I found her not breathing, I was to call for an ambulance.

"He informed me that no one would believe he'd done it because he would have a roomful of people swear he was with them in another state all day. Then I heard the house phone ring and saw him smile.

"He looked at his watch and said it was 'right on time.' He said that was his cell phone in Denver, calling here to talk to Caroline. When she didn't answer, of course, he would just hang up. That would polish off his alibi to perfection. He wasn't here and could prove it. He went on to say it was 'obvious' I was the guilty party if I even mentioned murder, so I had better keep my mouth shut.

"He got up, kicked me hard in the stomach, and walked away. I lay there for 15-20 minutes in such pain, both physical and mental. I cried hysterically for the baby I loved who was gone and for what it would do to Caroline. I wanted to die. Lying there, I wished he had killed me, too.

"After a while, the pain let up enough that I could crawl out of the room and pull myself up by the staircase banister. I slowly made it downstairs. I stared at the wall clock. Just waiting. When two hours were up, I called 9-1-1….

"She didn't have a mark on her and was certainly healthy and well fed, so they called it crib death. Just what he'd had in mind, I'm sure. No more baby, just like that. They didn't suspect foul play because my hysteria was real. My pain was out of control.

"After Henry murdered Cathleen, I knew he could get away with anything he wanted to. There was no stopping him. Whatever he wanted, he got. Rape, murder? It didn't matter. And whatever he didn't want was taken away.

"I tried to think of ways to get Caroline away from him but couldn't. She was already pretty turned off by him and his ignoring their child, anyway. They were sleeping in separate bedrooms. But it worried me that she was still in the same house."

Looking at her sister, Tracy said, "Caroline is the most incredible person I know. She has strength about her that no one can touch. She was a basket case after the baby died, for about a week. Then she pulled herself together and went on with her life. That's when she adopted Shana. Oh, you have no idea how mad that made Henry. But he couldn't tell her because he wasn't talking to her! I laughed over that a few times.

"They both knew the marriage was over by then, but Henry wasn't about to admit his marriage wasn't perfect. His life had to look perfect. Period. It wasn't an option.

"I avoided him like the plague. I never allowed myself to be in a room alone with him. I followed Caroline everywhere, even when she had to go to the bathroom! I know she thought I was getting needy all of a sudden.

"I got a new cell number and made sure Caroline memorized it and didn't write it down.

She didn't understand it, but she humored me.

"For the next three years or so, we seemed to be relatively safe. At least he was gone more and ignored us when he was home.

"The night I killed him, he just showed up at my apartment about seven. I didn't want to let him in, but he said through the door that, if I didn't, I would be very sorry. Since he could get away with murder, I knew he was right, and I let him in.

"He told me Caroline thought he was out of town. He said he planned to leave in the morning. I was scared out of my wits. The only other time he'd been in my apartment had left painful memories.

"Caroline called about seven-thirty and wanted to see if I could come over and have dinner with her and Shana. She said that Henry was out of town and that they were alone. With Henry standing right in front of me, I begged off saying I was really not feeling well. I told her I had eaten something that apparently had not agreed with me.

"Before I could get Caroline off the phone, I promised to go to the emergency room if I didn't get better. Food poisoning was nothing to play around with, she said. When I promised the second time, she hung up.

"I demanded to know what he was doing at my place. He was actually cordial and said he just needed someone to talk to. Yeah, right. Like I believed that! I poured us each a glass of wine after he requested it—certainly not the expensive stuff he'd brought all those years before, but he drank it.

"He said he hated that dumpy church that Caroline goes to. No one but losers went there. Henry said he'd figured out a way to get *rid* of it. Really! He said he'd figured out a way to get rid of the *church!* He said he was going to get it shut down!

"Henry then started bragging about how he'd gotten the security code to the church from, of all people, the pastor himself! A couple of weeks prior, he told me he went to the church on a Sunday morning, very early, before Caroline would arrive with Shana. He was the only one there when the pastor drove up and parked.

"He smirked at me, as he told of making a big deal to the pastor about having a question about something he read in the Bible. As if Henry would care about anything in that book.

"The pastor unlocked the door and went right for the security panel, with Henry on his heels, seemingly wanting answers. Pastor Tim was answering his question as he punched in the code, which Henry saw and memorized until he could write it down. He pulled a piece of paper out of the inside pocket of his jacket with the code on it, just to prove it to me.

"Henry told me that, when the pastor turned to look at him, he was staring out the window. He told the pastor his answer made perfect sense, and he was grateful for the help. He said Pastor Tim was delighted he was able to help a fellow Christian. Kinda makes you sick, doesn't it?

Anyway, Henry then told the Pastor he couldn't stay for services as he had to leave town on business. But Henry stressed he would have his Bible with him. Ha! Henry wasn't a Christian. He was the devil, himself.

"I got up and poured another glass of wine for us both. He continued to brag about how he'd always gotten what he wanted. Like I didn't already know that.

"I did ask him why he would want the code to the church, because that didn't make any sense to me. Henry said he was going to hide some drugs all over the building. Then there would be an anonymous call to the Feds. That would get the church shut down—maybe even get the pastor put in jail.

"Henry then started complaining about what a worthless wife he had and how he hated that brat Caroline had drug into his house. He asked for more wine. The more he drank, the angrier he got.

"Finally, he said he was going to have to

303

get rid of them—both, this time. He pulled a gun out of one coat pocket and a silencer out of the other. He smiled as he screwed the silencer onto the gun. He had it all figured out.

"Well, I went nuts and screamed at him! I told him he could not hurt my sister or my niece. Never would I allow that. Enough was enough. I wasn't going to take it anymore.

"That's when he looked at me as if it were the first time that night that he realized he was in the company of his wife's family.

"Then he started backtracking. He smiled and said he was just kidding, but I knew better. Henry had that calculating look on his face. He always did when he was planning evil stuff.

"He downed what was left of his drink and said he would pour the next glass. I became really scared. Memories of the last time this had happened flooded over me. Regular sex just didn't seem to do it for this creep—he had to abuse women.

"He was in the kitchen for what seemed a

long time, when I heard his cell ring. He stepped out of the kitchen, said he had to take this call, hurried into the bathroom, and shut the door. On his way there, he told me to just stay put until he was finished. It wouldn't take long.

"I slipped up to the closed bathroom door to listen but couldn't hear everything—just a few comments, but it was enough to scare me to death.

"I heard him say, 'Yeah, I know. I am going to take care of that. Tomorrow night, when she thinks I am out of town. No, don't worry. The sister did it. That's how it will look. Yeah. Okay, I'll be there late tomorrow night.' All I could hear was Henry's side of the conversation, of course, but the gist of it was pretty obvious.

"I had heard enough. He really was going to kill Caroline and Shana, and I would be blamed for their deaths! And I knew he would get away with it. He always did!

"I quietly left the bathroom door and went
305

into the kitchen where I found the two glasses full of wine. One was sitting farther away from the refrigerator than the other, and I figured that one was meant for me.

"I switched the glasses, putting them in the exact same position as I found them. I then tiptoed back into the living room and sat back down on the couch, in the same position and place I was before."

"Stop." Lou shut off the recorder and called a break before he left the room. Sometimes you just have to get away from the bad stuff.

"That's a really good idea, guys. Let's stand and stretch a moment." Donna was already out of her chair.

CHAPTER

24

After about ten minutes and refreshed with sodas or coffee, they were all seated again, and the recorder was clicked back on. Tracy continued where she'd left off.

"Like I said, I was sitting back on the couch just like I was when Henry had taken his phone call in the bathroom. He walked out of the bathroom when his call was finished. I could see from my peripheral vision that he glanced at me, but I continued to stare out the window. I wanted him to think I hadn't moved. It apparently worked.

"He walked into the kitchen, picked up the glasses, and delivered one to me.

"I told him I didn't want any more to drink. He hesitated a second and then told me he was sorry he'd said such a dumb thing. He said he didn't mean it. It must have just been the alcohol. We *had* drunk several already.

"I had to play the part, so I looked up at him and took my glass. He sat across the room again and drank his own wine. I watched him as casually as I could.

"I took a small sip of wine when Henry said, 'I'll bet I can empty mine before you can!'

"What a stupid thing to say. Did he really think I was that dumb? I guess so, but this wasn't his first glass, either, so I played along. I looked at him and gave a tiny smile. 'Yeah? Why not?'"

"We both started gulping down our wine, and we finished together. I really smiled now. The truth was about to come out. Either I drank out of the wrong glass and was about to be raped, lose what family I had left, and go to prison for life—or he was going to be heavily drugged. I knew I wouldn't have to wait long to figure out which."

Donna was the one who reached over and stopped the recorder this time. She was dumbfounded at what she was hearing and needed to get away from it for a moment.

"Sorry, break time again. There is something I have to do before we can go on. I'll be back in a moment." Donna left the room and headed for the lady's bathroom.

She walked the room for a few minutes, breathing deeply, trying to get her brain working again. The things she was hearing were unbelievable. What this woman had gone through! But Donna was a professional, and needed to get herself together and back in there.

Splashing cold water on her face helped.

When she went back, the others were still seated. She got settled, reached over to click the recorder on again, and nodded at Tracy.

"So, now would be the test as to which one of us was going to survive. About three minutes later, Henry had a big smile on his face. He got out of his chair to come over by me.

"About mid-room, he stopped. Obviously dizzy and disoriented, the shock was slow to find his face, but when it did, he glared at me with such hatred. I have to tell you, it was one of the most beautiful sights I have ever seen!

"He started talking. 'Why you dirty slu…. you switc…' Then he slumped to the floor.

"I removed the gun and silencer to put them in my purse, just in case he wasn't as out of it as he seemed.

"Outside was pitch black except for the occasional street light. Getting him into his car was difficult. I rolled him onto a blanket and slid him out! It was a bear, but I managed to get him sitting on the passenger's side. If I hadn't lived on the ground floor, I wouldn't have been able to do it. No doubt about it. I don't know, but I have to tell you, the adrenaline was pumping! I ran back to my apartment with the blanket, locked it inside, and then went back to his car.

"Not knowing what to do then, I drove away from the complex and parked in a closed gas station to think. There was no doubt in my mind by then: I was going to have to kill him! If I didn't, he would kill my sister and niece, and I would end up being blamed for it.

"There was one place I felt he needed to be when he died. Church. It needed to be the one he hated and wanted to get closed down. I reached into his jacket pocket and withdrew the security code. But how was I going to get the door open?

"I used to play games with my friends in college to see who could jimmy a lock the fastest. I didn't always win, but then, I didn't always lose, either. But I would need some kind of tool I didn't have.

"I made sure Henry was unconscious. Then I popped the trunk and went to look for something I could use to pick a lock with. What I found was unbelievable. Not only did I find any burglary tool I could possibly want, but there was a professional lock picker right there!

"That disgusting man was a filthy crook. He was ready for anything. I opened a suitcase that had clothes, extra ammo, and a gun case with another pistol in it. Anyway, I now had my way of getting through the church door.

"After driving him to the church just off South Seneca, he was now trying to return to consciousness. I had to be careful and move quickly. I used the lock pick tool and opened the church door without any trouble at all. I then shut off the alarm. It was dark, but that is the way I wanted it. Then I had to go back after Henry.

"Now, partially conscious, I was able to walk him inside. It wasn't easy as his knees kept buckling. After getting inside, he made it down the aisle only to the middle of the church. I wanted him to go all the way to the altar where he could face his Lord for the things had done to me and my sister, and I was sure, the many other people he had to have hurt along the way.

"Then I tried to pick him up a couple of times but wasn't strong enough. I started slapping his face, trying to get him to wake up. After a couple of moments, he did, at least a little. Groggy, he got up off the floor and stood, weaving back and forth.

"I knew he wouldn't make it any further up the aisle, so I got out the gun and connected the silencer. With the gun in my hands, I reached high for his temple. He tried, in his bleariness, to reach for the gun, and that is when I got my idea. Let him hold the gun. Let him pull the trigger on himself. Why not?

"So I wiped off the gun and silencer with my shirt, put the gun in his hand, put his finger on the trigger, and pointed it at his temple. I had to get on my tiptoes to reach, but I helped him pull the trigger. The bullet went into his brain with a soft 'puff' sound. Henry dropped, and the gun went under a seat somewhere. I didn't care where it had gone—it wasn't mine.

"I looked at him for just a second and then ran for the ladies room. I made sure the door was shut, and then I turned on the light. There aren't any windows in that room, so I wasn't worried about the light shining outside. I checked to make sure I wasn't covered in blood or something. I had some on my arm but not on my clothes—probably because I am so much shorter than him.

"Anyway, I cleaned myself up and left the church, closing the door behind me. I wiped his car off and his keys, so none of my prints would show. I then opened the trunk and removed fingerprints on the tools, the suitcase, and everything in it—anything that I had touched.

"When that was all done, I left on foot. Walking to Seneca Street, I headed north for about a mile or so, until I came to a QuikTrip and called a cab.

"The last thing I did was convince the cabby I had car trouble and would let my husband worry about it in the morning. He laughed and didn't ask any questions. Once back in my apartment, I cleaned up any sign of Henry being there and went to bed. I slept better that night than I had in years.

"That's it, detectives. The scumbag is dead."

The tape recorder was turned off. The room remained silent for several minutes before anyone spoke. Caroline held Tracy's hand the whole time.

Lou looked at Donna, who nodded slightly. He didn't want to do it, but he asked her to stand, and he put handcuffs on her, telling her she was being held the murder of Henry Wilkerson. She would be sent to the Sedgwick County Jail.

Caroline left, promising to have an attorney for her by morning. Donna hoped with all her heart she would. Quite frankly, she thought Tracy deserved a medal, not a jail sentence.

~~~

That night, Donna and Lou were at his mother's place for a steak dinner that Lou was grilling out on the patio. The night air was cold, but Lou said he didn't mind, and the truth of the matter was that he needed the alone time right now.

Inside, Donna was trying to make conversation because it was obvious Darlene knew they had tackled something at work that had them really down.

"It is so wonderful to see you again, Darlene. It has been such a long time! Last July wasn't it? That July 4th party by the pool?"

"It certainly was," Darlene said. "That was the occasion that Clarissa made such a scene about you being here that it ruined the party for everyone."

"Oh, no. I left so things would quiet down…"

"But it didn't. It got louder. Everyone was laying bets as to who would win!" Darlene had to chuckle.

"Oh, they did not! Really? Why would they keep arguing after I left? I thought my being there was the problem." Donna regretted the whole thing.

"Oh it *was* about you, alright. Lou had finally had enough and yelled so the whole neighborhood could hear, 'If you were half the woman Donna is, we wouldn't be having these discussions!'" Laughter came from the woman.

"Lou *said* that?" Donna was shocked. He'd taken up for her against his then-girlfriend.

"Oh, it wasn't the first time! I remember…."

~~~

317

Lou could see the giggling of the women inside and was glad there was something to laugh about. The day had been rough. He loved being a cop, but the thought of that Tracy girl going to prison for life for killing a pig like Wilkerson… Well, it had his guts in a knot.

Donna felt the same. He knew she did. You could see it on her face. That beautiful face should never have to see injustice like this. He knew he felt really protective of his partner, but he couldn't tell her that. She would dump him in a heartbeat. A partner has to have your back, and personal feelings can't be involved. But he knew he would never let anything happen to her. He would take ten bullets before he would let one hit her.

He could see the steaks were perfect. Lou loaded them on the platter and walked in to find his mother and Donna smiling straight at him.

"Whaaaat?"

All Darlene and Donna could do was laugh.

CHAPTER

25

The whole idea of Tracy going on trial for murder was offensive to Donna. It was self-defense, plain as day! There was no doubt in anyone's mind that Caroline would get her the best lawyer money could buy, and that gave some degree of comfort, but even to have to *go* through a trial was a disgrace.

Donna and her partner had an appointment with the captain late in the morning to go over every detail. What would be done with this was anyone's guess. Tracy hadn't been officially charged with anything yet, but she had been put in county lockup since her confession the day before.

There were so many charges that could be filed, and, then again, those same charges could be argued for the defense.

"Your Honor, there is the charge of breaking and entering the church."

"Your Honor, no one has pressed charges for her entering the church. In fact, the pastor said she could enter the church whenever she wanted to!"

"Your Honor, we have a murder on our hands. Mr. Wilkerson is dead."

"Your Honor, God himself said it is not murder to kill the guilty! Would the Prosecution tell God He is a liar?"

Donna kept throwing these barbs through her mind as she was watching the clock tick the minutes away until their meeting with Captain

Parry. Never could she remember the time going so slowly.

"Your Honor, the charge of drugging and kidnapping a man is a serious one."

"Your Honor, the Prosecution is putting words in the dead man's mouth. How do we know that he didn't want to go to the church? He spoke of wanting to! As far as being drugged, did he not bring the drugs himself? Of course, he was planning to take them!"

"Your hon...."

"Decker, McGregor, get in here!" Parry stuck his head out of his office and disappeared back into it just as fast.

"Finally." Lou muttered. Donna nodded as they rushed to their destination.

"Sit, sit." Parry pointed out the chairs as he shut the door behind them.

When he sat back down, it was more of a slump than a conscious act. Seeing that their captain was not exactly happy with this case was somewhat disturbing.

"Okay, here is what we have. I might add up front that all of this has been given to both Tracy's new attorney, Derrick Porter, and District Attorney Clark. Clark said that he would go over the file and that his decision would be made today. Obviously Tracy's attorney wanted her out of lockup, but Clark said it could wait until he made his decision. That was about an hour ago. He will be making a statement for the press at three this afternoon. We will know when the whole world knows."

"How does it look?" Lou couldn't stop clenching his jaw.

"How does it look? The woman confessed to drugging and killing the man. How do you *think* it looks?" Parry was definitely irritated. "I'm sorry, Lou. I don't mean to get pissed off. This case just gets to me. I talked to Clark for more than two hours last night. I let him know we didn't think this woman's reputation, let alone her life, should be ruined over swine like this."

Both Lou and Donna expressed the same feelings.

"What are the options, Captain?" Donna wanted to know where Tracy stood.

"Well, she could be charged with each individual crime she committed; the drugging, the kidnapping, breaking and entering, murder, the whole bit. But we have a couple of things that may break that up."

Lou jumped on that one, "What do you mean, break it up?"

"Well, the DA won't be able to prove that she drugged him."

"I don't understand," said Donna. "She admitted to it."

Parry smiled at that one. "We only have her *word* for that. We can't prove she did it! The GHB was completely gone from his system by the time of the autopsy. We have no way of knowing if it was ever there. We only have her word for it." They all smiled.

"Plus, if he did ingest it, if he brought it, if he had put it in the wine, and if he drank it, he must have wanted to ingest it." All of them were enjoying the captain's take on the charges.

"Then there's the kidnapping. Wilkerson could have told her to drive him to the church! We don't know he didn't want to be there. We just have…"

"*HER WORD FOR IT!*" All three of them finished the sentence. With the resulting chuckles, some of the tension in the room was gone.

"Yeah, but then there is the murder…," Donna threw that one out there.

"Yeah, there's that. We are kinda stuck there. The D.A. won't have the option of dropping it down to manslaughter because it was premeditated." Parry slammed his pencil down onto his desk. "If anyone deserves to have a bullet in his head, it is that sorry piece of…."

"But none of her prints were found. Not

one! There is nothing to show she was even there, except…" Donna's mind was moving a mile a minute, going over the crime scene again and again.

"Yeah, 'her word for it.' Don't take that lightly, guys. That confession is about as damaging as it can get."

Gloom entered the room again.

"Get out of here. Keep yourselves busy. I'll turn on the TV for Clark's decision."

They didn't have to be told twice.

~~~

Everyone in the squad room was waiting for the D.A.'s announcement at three. Some ran to get work done so they could be back to watch it; others made deals with others to call them immediately. This case had made national news

325

because it crossed so many state lines. The news media couldn't get enough of Wilkerson.

Lou went and picked up burgers and fries for everyone, and he ate quietly with his partner at their desks.

At two-thirty, Lou whispered to her, "What do you think will happen?"

Donna looked up at him and shook her head. "Clark is a good man. Everyone knows that. But we also know he plays by the law. A murder is pretty hard to ignore."

"Yeah. I hear ya. I don't like it, but I hear ya."

At ten till the hour, Parry came out of his office and turned on the fifty-five-inch flat screen attached to the wall. He adjusted it until he had KWCH, Channel 12 on. Every person there grew silent and was walking up to be close. Donna and Lou were no different. They stood silent as the clock's second hand ticked… and ticked, as the moments went by ever so slowly.

About six minutes later, a news break

came on, and Donna gasped when she saw Cassie Harper's face.

"Thank you, Angela. Yes, I am here just outside the courthouse waiting for District Attorney Harlan Clark to share his decision concerning Tracy Andrew's future over the death of Henry Wilkerson.

"As we wait, let's go over some of the details as we know them. Three weeks ago, Henry Wilkerson was found dead in the Trinity Pentecostal Church, just off of South Seneca here in Wichita. He had been shot in the head, and the gun was found near his body."

"Sorry to interrupt you, Cassie," said the current news anchor, Angela Farlow. "I have a quick question. Didn't they find that the security system had been shut off? That someone knew the code?"

"Yes, that is correct, Angela. The front door lock had been jimmied, and the security code turned off. That was one of the initial problems surrounding this case. How did the deceased get the code to the church? The pastor, Tim Stanton, said he had no idea as it was very privileged information. Tracy Andrews later stated that Wilkerson told her the code had been obtained from the pastor himself, but, of course, without his knowledge.

"Stanton found the body when he…Oh, here comes the D.A. now, Angela. We are finally going to get a decision. Stay with me as I get closer!" Cassie moved up to within two feet of Clark as he stood on the courthouse steps, in front of a podium that had just been set down.

In the squad room, you could hear a pin drop. Donna wasn't even aware that she was holding her breath.

The courthouse was going crazy with the news media that had converged upon the city in such a short period of time.

"Clark, what are you…," "Mr. District Attorney, have you decided to…," "Is it homicide, Clark?" "Did Tracy do it?" "What are you…?"

DONALIE BELTRAN

Raising his hands to quiet the crowd, Harlan Clark stood silently for a long moment. Donna thought her heart would stop.

"Ladies and gentlemen…, this has been a very difficult case. I want to thank the Wichita Police Department and especially Captain George Parry for doing such a fine job of investigating this case. We all know it has not been easy.

"As you know by now, Wichita businessman Henry Wilkerson was found dead in a local church, with the gun that killed him lying a few feet away. The initial problem was to figure out if the death was a murder or a suicide." Clark took another long moment to shuffle some papers in front of him. Then stared at the ground until he'd gathered his thoughts.

"And, as you also know, Tracy Andrews, the widow's sister, came forward and confessed to killing Wilkerson."

"Is it murder, Clark?" "Did she drag…?" "Who opened the…?"

329

Clark stood silent, waiting for the new buzz to die down before continuing. When they saw he would not continue until they stopped, everyone quieted down again.

"After investigating all angles of this case, going through all the evidence, researching the law, and after having Tracy Andrews seen by our psychiatrist… It is the judgment of this department that… that this death was indeed a suicide."

The entire squad room erupted into clapping and hollering. Lou yelled for everyone to be quiet so they could hear the rest. Stunned, Donna didn't say a word but was actually able to breathe again.

Clark didn't miss a beat. "We feel Tracy Andrews was experiencing a nervous breakdown when she confessed to the death. Tracy has a very close relationship with her sister, almost maternal in her need to protect the sister. Tracy was present when her sister's baby died of crib death, and we believe the loss of her sister's husband only pushed her further over the edge, leaving her feeling guilt for her sister's pain.

"We have discovered Wilkerson led a less-than-honorable life, and we believe he finally couldn't handle it any more. Maybe he knew his time was up or that there was a price on his head. We will never know for sure, of course, but we do know he died of his own hand.

"Further, Ms. Andrews' statements could not be confirmed with any kind of evidence at all. No fingerprints, DNA, nothing. Everything she had told the police could not be corroborated in any way. Without any evidence to show her involvement, it leads me to believe it was all fabricated in her confused mind.

"The police were able to locate her about a mile from the scene, at approximately the time of the death. Being a mile from a crime scene in this city is hardly reason to prosecute! If it were, I would probably be in jail myself."

The media reporters chuckled with him.

"Sir, what about the gun found in the church?"

"It was not found to be involved in any other crime. It was not registered, however, but we have no reason to believe it was not Mr. Wilkerson's."

"What about the drugs that were supposedly given to him?

Clark replied, "There was no evidence of any drugs in his system from the autopsy."

"But the autopsy wasn't done for two days after his death. Couldn't it have been there and gone by the time tests were taken?"

"Anything is possible, but, as I said, no drugs were in his system, and if any were there at the time of death, it can't be proven," Clark said.

"We searched Tracy's apartment and found no evidence that the dead man had *ever* been there. There were no prints, DNA, or anything else to show his presence, despite Tracy's statement that he was.

"As you can see, the entire statement she made does not hold water. None of it. Henry

Wilkerson killed himself."

"Mr. Clark, what about...?

Parry turned off the TV, looked at his crew, and growled, "Get back to work! This isn't your day off!"

Everyone scattered.

MURDER FOR A MOMENT

CHAPTER

26

It was Thanksgiving Day. The Henry Wilkerson case had been closed for a couple of weeks. Lou and Donna had been assigned another case, and this one was obviously a murder. But they weren't going to worry about it today.

It seemed everyone who had been involved in the case of Henry's death had been invited to Caroline Wilkerson's for the holiday dinner.

Lou and Darlene arrived just behind Donna and her parents, Brad and Betty Decker. Donna loved hearing those glorious doorbell chimes again. Her brother, Roy Decker, his wife, Louise, and their children were spending the holiday at his in-laws in Oklahoma, or they would have come as well.

Caroline opened the door, saw them all standing there, and hollered, "Get in here out of the cold. All of you! You'll freeze!" It *was* a cold day, about thirty degrees. Very typical Wichita in late November.

Caroline gave Donna a big hug, then ushered in Lou and Darlene. She then turned to the rest of her guests and announced, "Donna and Lou are here, *finally!*" Everyone cheered, and their parents were introduced to more cheers.

"Well, I would have been on time," Darlene said with a grin at Lou, "but my son here couldn't decide if he wanted to wear the gray pin-stripe with the burgundy tie or the navy suit with the yellow tie. I thought I would have to dress him myself!"

Lou turned crimson and shrugged. "What's a man to do when he wants to look good?" He took the laughter in stride.

"I agree with you totally, my friend!" It was Pastor Stanton. There was no doubt that he shared the same desire to dress as well as Lou.

Lily looked at Donna and said, "When it comes to Tim getting dressed, I could tell you stories you wouldn't believe!" Everyone laughed at her comment, even the men.

"Where's Gabe?" Donna glanced around the crowd.

"Oh, he'll be here in a moment. He had to stop and pick up Stella. You can't find one without the other!" Then Lily leaned in so only Donna could hear and whispered, "I think this Christmas, Stella may have more jewelry to wear... I'm just saying..."

Donna opened her mouth and eyes wide and just hugged Lily! *How wonderful for them both*, she thought. *Stella will make the perfect wife for him.*

Lily went on, "We even tried to get Hawk to come with us today, but he refused. Said he didn't have any decent clothes and would feel out of place. I spoke with Caroline, and she is going to box up a bunch of the leftovers and send it to him. It will be enough to hold him for three days or more!" It was obvious the addition of Hawk to the family was not a problem for these wonderful people.

The whole party was for what Caroline described as the ones who "made my life a joy." Present was their boss, George Parry, and his wife, JoAnne, as well as Tracy's attorney, Derrick Porter. They mingled, knowing a lot of the people present and introducing themselves to those they didn't. Miles had been invited but he was hosting his own family get-together with his wife.

Just when it was time to sit down to dinner, Gabe and Stella arrived to jokes about their tardiness.

It was Pastor Tim who said, "I am not going to ask you what you were doing that made you late. But I have to say, that color lipstick looks great on you, son!"

Stella laughed along with everyone else while an embarrassed Gabe went to the hall bathroom to take care of the problem.

Caroline had spared no expense in throwing this dinner for a couple dozen people, in celebration for the holiday and all that she had to be thankful for. Amazingly, her huge dining area had room for everyone and then some. She'd invited each and every person who played a part in getting to the truth about her husband's death. Whatever that truth might be, she didn't care. Some had to decline her invitation due to their family obligations, but many were there.

Due to what the court said was her false testimony to police, Tracy had been court-ordered to two weeks of psychotherapy and was now living with Caroline and Shana. She had taken over the second master suite that Caroline and Shana used to live in.

With the court order already ended, she decided to continue with a therapist to help her put the past behind her. She was writing a book about her ordeal entitled, "My Escape From Hell."

When Donna spotted Tracy, she rushed to hug her.

"How wonderful to see you again, Tracy." Donna was just bubbling at the thought that Tracy had not been put through more hell over Wilkerson.

"Not *nearly* as wonderful as seeing your beautiful face again!" Tracy was so happy, she looked like she could float.

The party had been catered, so Heddy and all of her children were there as guests. The place was filled with love and laughter.

Donna and Lou stayed together most of the time. Both were so glad at the rare happy ending to such tragedies. The soft background music was old-time gospel that brought back wonderful memories for her.

It was music she loved, so Donna hummed along from time to time. She would find Lou smiling at her when she did, which made her blush. He even held her hand for a few moments.

Donna's parents were having a wonderful time with everyone. Laughter was everywhere. *What a happy home this has become. And to think of what it was…*

After dinner, everyone was lounging around in groups talking about the upcoming holidays. Just when she didn't think the day could get any better, the door chimes rang.

Heddy made it to the door first and opened it. In walked Cassie Harper, looking radiant as usual. When the guests saw her, everyone became quiet, and those standing moved back toward the walls, opening up the room for Caroline.

From the dining room, Caroline held Shana's hand and walked through the living room and into the entry foyer, right next to her new guest.

Cassie was staring at the gorgeous little girl with the long dark hair and eyes as blue as… well, as blue as Jackie's.

Caroline said, "Shana, I would like to introduce you to your Aunt Cassandra…."

~~~~~~~~~~~~~~~~~~~~~~~~~~~~~~~

I truly hope you enjoyed reading MURDER FOR A MOMENT.

If you did, please go to Amazon.com and leave a review.

Thank you and God Bless,

Donalie